A DOVE OF T...
STORIES

"A first-rate collection by a writer with a remarkably fresh sensibility . . . everywhere rich and evocative."

—Chaim Potok

"A wonderful writer. He moves from character to character and from culture to culture, as if he'd been born and raised everywhere. . . . The book is a joy to come across."

—John Gardner

"Helprin writes like a saint, plots like a demon, and has an imagination that would be felonious in all but the largest democracies."

—*The Village Voice*

"Haunting stories by a fresh and accomplished writer who seems at ease, whatever his subject, whatever his setting, whatever his time."

—*Publishers Weekly*

Other Books by Mark Helprin

REFINER'S FIRE
ELLIS ISLAND & OTHER STORIES
WINTER'S TALE

A DOVE OF THE EAST
EAST
& Other Stories

Mark Helprin

A LAUREL BOOK
Published by
Dell Publishing Co., Inc.
1 Dag Hammarskjold Plaza
New York, New York 10017

FOR
THEODORE MORRISON

Amor mi mosse, che mi fa parlare.
—INF. II

CONTENTS

A DOVE OF THE EAST

A Jew of Persia

He had tried to explain for his sons the sense of mountains so high, sharp, and bare that winds blew ice into waves and silver crowns, of air so thin and cold it tattooed the skin and lungs with the blue of heaven and the bronze of sunshining rock crevasse. He had tried to tell them of the house in which he had lived, made of mountain rock, with terraces, and ten fires within—when shutters were thrown open and hit the stone like the report of a shell in an echoing valley he could see mountains of white ice two hundred miles distant. The eggs there were milk-white, the milk like cloud. In winter it often snowed in one day enough to trap and kill horses and bulls. He had been a sawyer, guiding his saws through countless timbers all day long in the open air, so that his body was as intensely powerful as (he would say) gun-powder in a brass casing. Then, when he was younger and worked at the timbers, he could

by the pressure of his hands and arms break a heavy
iron chain. And there was not much else, at least as
he thought of it twenty and more years later. These
things were so deep and wonderful that they could
bear telling a thousand times a thousand times. But
he could not say them even once to his sons, for they
did not know Persian, which he had almost forgotten,
and his Hebrew was of the shacks and hot streets and
blood-guttered markets.

This life of his came to be like the fall of an angel,
and yet by the tenets of his belief he believed himself
lucky. He had come alone from Persia's mountainous
north, where the air was cross-currented and sym-
phonically clear, to Tel Aviv where air was obsolete
and the entire city heated like potters' kilns in Iran.
When in late 1948 he had stepped off a small ship in
Jaffa, he had said to himself, Najime, it will be profit-
able to find the large oven which heats up the city,
for there they are undoubtedly drying vast amounts
of wood, and may need me to saw. For several hours
he had glided about the city in his boots of fur and
leather asking passers-by in Persian, "Where is the
great oven?" The passers-by, obviously ignorant of
Persian, jaded by the sight of ambulant wolflike luna-
tic-looking Persians and Turcomans, would throw up
their hands, shrug their shoulders, and say to themselves in Yiddish, He should only not kill me dear
God. And Najime would continue on, still in search
of the all-pervasive heat.

Instead of his crooked, ancient, and vast stone
house with ether forcing its way shrieking through
the cracks, and fires flickering, instead of sheepskins
and earthenware pitchers of iced white wine, instead

of the little synagogue where sawyers, sheepherders, and merchants watched the sun rise golden from a cradle of distant mountains and light gold chains coming triangularly from the ceiling, instead of tall candles, and contests of strength in the bitter cold, he found a tin shack almost melting, filthy sacks for a bed, no breeze, rationed food, a synagogue of brown Yemenites and Moroccans who were softer and soaking in Arabic and the desert and knowing a God who possessed another face than his rugged, whistling, clean, and mystic God of altitudes, hunters, and eagles' flight. That was the angel's fall, and he often inflated himself with longing, letting the remaining Persian words circle around by themselves in his head, reluctant to talk to others whose dialects were not the same.

But his balance on the scaffolded logs had long before taught him of polarities, and he was well aware of the blessings of his situation. To his eldest son Yacov he had often said, There is plenty of balance here for what was lost. Of course he knew that the boy, knowing no other country, brought up as it were in a sewing box, would never sense except in the airy sadness of dreams what Persia had been like, and that since he had become a sergeant in the army and had been in battles he had learned his own lessons and only tolerated his strange father, although he loved him, for his father was a rough peasant who had walked halfway across Asia from deep in the past, and the young man already had a small car and a telephone of his own. But Najime went on anyway, as he often did, saying, "There are two main things which balance out the loss, two main things. The first is that

I have come to a Jewish country where I can live as a Jew (although you know I lived as a Jew there too), and have helped to build the third commonwealth, a new land for us. The soldiers I see are our soldiers, and that is good, and Hebrew is our language. That is good." He stopped, beaming, and poured himself a glass of grapefruit juice from an old bottle. His son looked at him with an habitual incredulousness.

"Nu?" said the stocky ex-sergeant. "And . . . ?"

"That's all," said Najime, "what else?"

"What is the second reason? You said there were two."

"I can't tell you."

"Why not?"

"I can't say."

"Nonsense," said Yacov, slamming the table with his fist. "You always say there are two reasons and then give only one."

"I know," said Najime, strangely upset, then re-treating into his thoughts and memories like an old man.

"You are *not* such an old man, you know. You can't do this. What is the second reason? I know. You can't tell me."

They had had this exchange a hundred times a hundred times, and always with the same result. But once at a wedding Najime had consumed three bottles of wine. Then when his son had pressed him for the second reason he had blurred out, "Because I saw the Devil, and he had fur in his eyes." He had started to shake, and the boy in the new uniform had seen the hair on his father's arms and neck stand up. What did he mean? Certainly he had not seen the Devil.

But from then on he would elaborate no further, and any inquiry about (directly) the Devil, or (indirectly in order, he thought, subtly to pry out the secret) the strange condition of having fur in the eyes, brought Yacov a hard slap in the face and a long stream of expletives in mountain Persian.

And so they had continued to live out their lives in the Ha Tikva Quarter, a place where all the functions of human existence combined ungraciously and people were struck like bells in no chorus, camel bells upset and sad but active in contrast to the still green palms, a tree with a lisp in the wind and infinite patience, variegated sun shadows, shelterer of doves, the green rafters of Tel Aviv. All this in the Ha Tikva was sometimes struck down by the Hamsin, and more significantly, sometimes blown onto another course by winds of war and death and change. And at these times the inhabitants paused in the struggle, and very like sailors on a coasting ship breaching a passage of high cliffs and tumultuous blue-green waters into an unknown gulf or sea, waited for the change, marking into an unknown gulf or sea, waited for the change, marking a point in their lives, aware of time and their part in it. And one day this violent wind was blowing through Ha Tikva, at least for Najime and his son.

Najime was sitting on his chair, listening to the BBC Arabic service (of which he understood nothing) and looking out onto the street. In the distance he saw the tops of a few skyscrapers, and closer, a row of palms which caught a sea breeze never to reach him. Closer still was a series of old concrete buildings which had been built with sea water a generation or

more before and which like lepers had been losing
bits and pieces ever since. Before him was a street
of hard-packed dust lined with sterile date palms, tin
shacks, dogs, and chickens. Yacov was sitting in the
back of the room cleaning a submachine gun he had
stolen from the army. He had its various parts and
springs assembled unassembled before him ready to
be oiled, and was about to begin work on the magazines when he was startled by the crash of his father's
chair.

Najime had crouched like a hunter among the
rocks, and was staring out the window, jaw hanging
open. "What is it!" screamed Yacov, as he like the
trained soldier he was vaulted over the kitchen table
to his father's side, wincing in mid-air as he heard the
several dozen springs, nuts, and molded pieces of his
gun jangle onto the floor.

"It's him."

"Who?" said Yacov, staring in terrified sympathy
at the familiar street.

"That man. The one with the flat chin and
half-grown beard."

"That little guy?"

"Yes."

"Well what about him? What's with you? Are you
crazy?"

The little old man on the street, in appearance a
cross between a beggar and a mushroom, turned into
an alley and vanished. Yacov glanced at the metal
pieces on the floor and then at his father. He was dis-
gusted and perplexed. But his father's wells had been
tapped. He picked up his son and threw him across

the room onto the bed, ran to close the shutters, bolted the door, and stood there in chevrons of light.

"You dog-headed baby, you cackling jackass. What do you know! Now listen, because the time has come. I was afraid of it for twenty-five years, but it stares me in the face at last and I feel like dying, and that is the only way to enter a fight. I will fight," he said, upraising a still very strong arm, "and I will die, but I will use sword and dagger until they heat from friction in the air. The dust will rise about me. I will be fierce."

"What are you talking about?" said Yacov, who was himself now terrified like a child whose father is in danger. The older man sat down, and after a short silence, began to speak in determined vision of the past.

"I was a young man, the strongest in the village, at least among the Jews, because I sawed beams all day and had done so from the earliest I could remember. Because of that I had great lungs, great balance, and great muscular power. I was a skilled swordsman too, for there was no sword in the world which was not to me as light as a feather compared to my saws, sledgehammers, and axes. I could run for half a day at a time up and down the valleys, and raise beams alone which five men together would not approach. Naturally, I won most of the contests.

"One day a messenger came from the Grand Rabbi in the capital. In the presence of our Rabbi and the elders he commanded us to collect our gold, our silver, our jewels, our coins, and bring them to him in the capital on an appointed day. He said that the Jews of the world were in the midst of returning, that the ingathering of the exiles was about to begin, that all the Jews of Iran, and India, the East, and the West, were giving their treasure. You can imagine how it struck us. Two thousand years, and at last we were leaving our beloved mountains for the land of our fathers.

"Although we were rich in many things and close to God, we were nevertheless a poor village. All of our gold and silver including everything from the synagogue itself filled only one sack on a donkey. On the other side, to balance the load, we placed a sack of dried and smoked meats, cheeses, and dried fruits. I was to go alone in order not to attract attention, but fully armed, as there were many bandits in those mountains at the time, and probably still are. I had the finest sword and dagger in the village. We attempted to borrow a rifle from the Muslims, but they would not hear of it. On top of the sacks we put false containers which made it seem as if we had a donkey loaded with dried dung. I was dressed poorly, my weapons hidden. After a good night's sleep and a meal, I set out.

"Three days from our village and any other I arrived at a great pass in the mountains, to which I had been only once before, as a child. This pass is essentially a vast gorge with paths cut into the rock walls on either side. Once you have chosen a side you must stay with it until the end, about an hour's travel, because a sane donkey would not walk backwards with no room to turn. The other path is completely inaccessible although only a stone's throw distant, because the gorge in between it easily a kilometer deep. It was this pass which kept the railways, armies, and telegraphs from our village. It was this barrier which allowed us to follow our own desires freely, and yet because of it the bandits were also free and they plagued us.

"But no bandit had ever struck there, simply because were he to have done so and encountered greater force he would have had no way to escape, and besides, the place was dangerous enough just to traverse. At the end of the pass was a government station full of troops. So if one reached the entrance he assumed himself safe from attack. Naturally the troops themselves exacted a small extra-legal tax, but that was looked upon as inevitable, as a sort of toll.

"I found myself at the entrance to the pass, thinking I was safe from bandits and even exempt from the soldiers' 'tax.' If the Grand Rabbi had treasure coming to him from all parts of the country, he had undoubtedly donated part of it to an official in the palace to make sure that it arrived intact. My donkey had a bad right eye, which was lucky for me. My natural inclination was to travel on the left, with the gorge on my right, and since the animal's left eye was best, that is what we were forced to do. I made sure the sacks were evenly balanced, put a blinder on his right eye so that he would look only at the path, and said a prayer. Then I led him out.

"We were doing well, and the animal's brown legs were steady and not shaking as they would have done had he been other than a donkey and smart enough to fear heights. Halfway through I saw two men, one on each path. They were bandits, and each one had a rifle. How clever they were! The one on the far side trained his rifle on me, while the other calmly awaited my approach. What have you got there, Jew, said the one closest to me. Just dung for fires, I said. (I must also have said sir.)

"He believed me, and was going to let me pass when the other one, on the far side, said, Look in his sacks, little brother, for I think there is gold there. It seemed very strange that he should know that, and he too was rather strange. Even from that distance I sensed something about him which frightened me, and the donkey was very agitated in his presence. Well, they thought they had the mastery of design in that matter, but they hadn't. Perhaps if I had been carrying just smoked meats or tools or my own money, I would not have been able to think out a way to beat them. There were after all two of them, each with a rifle and a knife. I had only a sword and dagger. And most important, I could do nothing to the older one across the gorge who in complete safety had his rifle aimed at my heart. Even were he not there I could not have gone in any but one direction, straight into his little brother, who was by no means little. But I was carrying the wealth of my father and my father's father, and of all my cousins, and of the synagogue in the village. And it was for a very special purpose, very special indeed, so I thought so hard my head began to boil and the veins in my hands stood out. (I was also quite frightened.)

"After I had thought of what to do it seemed so simple and obvious that I laughed out loud, and it echoed in the gorge. They looked at one another in confusion, but then the older one said, Little brother, we can also rob madmen. Then the little brother ordered me to spill out my sacks for him. No sir, I said, you cannot make me do that, even if you kill me. If I am to be robbed that is one thing, robbing myself is another.

"He thought for a while and then said, That makes sense, Jew, and then very casually went to the sack of dried fruits and meats and began to go through it. You see he was not afraid of me because I was a Jew. When you say 'I am a Jew,' they think you are weak. But of course we are as strong as anyone else, and because of that we often give them big surprises. Afterwards they hate us because they think we have tricked them. But usually it is they who have tricked themselves. Their eyes have done the tricking. As soon as little brother saw my clothing he lost all fear, because knowing that I was a Jew he did not think there was a man underneath.

"He has false sacks of dung, he yelled to his brother, and then began to lay out the meat and fruit against the wall of the path next to the donkey. I knew exactly what to do; it had come to me in a flash. I came close to him and said, Keep the meat and fruit, eat well, but in God's mercy let me pass. He looked up and said, I am going to eat well, but I am also going to kill you, for if I don't kill you I will have no appetite, and he laughed.

"At this I imagined as best I could that he was a branch on a long timber which awaited trimming before being sawed into logs. How many tens of thousands of times I had knocked off those thick branches with one stroke of my ax. But it was different with a man. I had never killed a man, and I found that I could not move. I was paralyzed. Then I realized that I could not fool myself into imagining that he was a branch to be severed, because he clearly was a man. So I thought, This is a man, not a tree, and I am going to kill him. I was afraid, and I knew that the minute I reached for my sword all hell would break out. I knew that if I hesitated they would kill me, and that if I did nothing they would kill me. This made me so angry that I pulled out my sword and with the most powerful stroke I had ever given (and the fastest), ten times as powerful as was necessary, I simply cut him in half.

"I dropped my sword immediately and grabbed the lower half of his body, throwing it with all my might over into the gorge. Meanwhile his brother had begun firing his rifle and had hit my donkey, who went down on one knee. I could not stand the idea of having the body of the man I had just killed next to me, so at further risk of losing all the gold and my life I picked it up and sent it flying in a wide arc into the gorge. It seemed to hang motionless at the top of the arc, and since the other had stopped firing in his horror at this I had time to grab the faltering donkey and pull him back onto the path. Then the big brother began to fire many bullets, quite accurately I must admit, but they all went into the poor dead animal in front of me. He was smart though, because he began firing into the rocks, which broke into shrapnel and bloodied me all up. I took a silver bowl and some trays from the sacks and put it over my head and them over my body, remaining there quite comfortably for another half hour eating lamb and pears and wincing at each shot and ricochet. Then he stopped, thinking either that I was dead, or that if I were not he wasn't going to change the situation.

"I looked at him through a little space between the donkey's neck and the ground, and I cannot adequately describe what I saw. I was not afraid of him until that point, because I had planned to stay there until dark and then carry the treasure to the army station. Were he to move back to where I had begun he would have given me an hour's head start, during which I could easily get to the army base. Were he to wait until dark, the darkness would shield me from his fire. I knew he could not go forward for fear that the troops ahead would kill him, so you see I had turned what they believed to be their great advantage, the safety of the gorge, into *my* great advantage. And I was unafraid, until I looked under the curve of the donkey's neck and saw big brother.

"What had been a simple ordinary bandit was suddenly something most different. I could not believe my eyes, and rubbed them. *His* eyes were red circular coals, but made of fur, and they flashed and glowed. His chin had extended until it looked like the flat wooden pallet bakers use for taking bread out of the oven, and he was foaming at the mouth. Up and down the rock walls sparks flew, and as he gesticulated and mouthed the words of evil animals a hot wind came through the crevasse, and hot drops of rain, and then thunder. The wind, at least it seemed to me, was trying to blow the donkey's body off the path. The more big brother danced and fumed, the higher the wind became and the more the donkey moved bit by bit, almost imperceptibly. After a while big brother seemed to get tired, the wind died down, and darkness began to fall. Then he seemed to be like a bandit again, with the almost pitiful exaggerated half-bearded chin, and he called out to me: I am going to hunt you down and cut your throat with a razor. I will follow you anywhere on earth, in these mountains, on the seas, in cities, anywhere. I will strike when you think you are safe and comfortable. I can walk through walls—nothing can keep me out—and when I cut your throat I will be laughing and wild with pleasure, and you will be frozen like a board, unable to move as the razor glides. I can do that. You know me, and your life will be far worse than your death, which will be a well of terror.

"Well, I don't scare that easily, so when darkness fell I cut the treasure from the donkey and pushed him off the ledge, as if to bury him. I heard a hissing of air as he fell into the blue-black darkness. Then, even though it was dark, I almost ran over that path all the way to the army station. I dared not tell them what had happened for fear that they would go mad (those peasant soldiers living alone in mountaintops were really crazy, believe me), but they took me in for a night.

"You don't believe that they were really crazy? They spent hours slapping each other's faces. They moaned and whimpered like dogs. They used to go around on stilts to scare away devils. This is not crazy?"

By this time it was dark: no more light came in through the louvres, and the old man had been talking into the night for longer than he thought. Yacov reached out to touch him as if to make sure he were really there, then got up to turn on the light, which blinded them both. Surely this was something his father had imagined long ago on a terrifying day and night in the mountains, and yet even if not entirely consistent, it was convincing. With the excitement of a fool who knows one small thing, Yacov asked his father, "If he were really the Devil, why could he not have flown across the gorge on the wind and killed you with his teeth, or have sent a snake from above to poison you?"

"He wasn't the Devil. He was only a half devil, perhaps the son of the Devil and a human woman. He had powers, but they were limited. That is why he has grown old, and why I was able to beat him. Very few men, at least not the likes of me, can beat the Devil. But one of his sons, well, that's different."

"How can you be sure he knows you are here?"

"Because *he* is here."

"Well, I think we should wait and see what happens. Maybe it's nothing at all. Maybe we are dreaming."

"Of course my son," said Najime, "of course we'll wait, that's part of it." He expected the weeks to pass, and they did.

Meanwhile, stories had been spreading about the newcomer. It seems he had arrived from nowhere with a large wagon full of the finest avocados. Since avocados were out of season, he sold them at a very high price and was almost immediately transformed from beggar to prosperous merchant. When people asked him, as they did, where he had gotten so many thousands of avocados he said that his brother had a farm in the desert, where it was so hot that he could grow anything he wanted year round, even at night. It was said that beggars were envious of him, a beggar become rich, and so spread stories such as the one asserting that he sold avocados from his wagon for two weeks day and night and never seemed to run out.

A hundred men threw themselves at his feet and begged to buy his wagon. He picked the richest of them all and told him to run and get his daughter. When the man returned with the beautiful young girl she went wild with desire for the hideous old man and asked for his wrinkled hand in marriage. With tears in his eyes, the father gave consent. They were married the next day. Twenty-five minutes after the wedding feast the father died suddenly of what an autopsy later revealed as starvation.

The stranger then moved into the family house, sold it that evening at a great profit even though everyone knew the city was about to tear it down to build a melon exchange, and pooled his considerable assets to buy up all the salt in Tel Aviv. This was considered a foolish move, until several days later when news came from the south that the country's salt mines had become filled with hot poisonous gas from fissures in the earth. The salt merchants got together and put all their capital into a large order of Turkish salt to be brought on a ship they purchased as a consortium. News came that the ship had been sunk by the Lebanese. The stranger bought what remained of their businesses for practically nothing, and went to the docks to meet the ship, which had not been sunk, but had doubled in size.

From this point, his dealings became unknown to the people of Ha Tikva, except that it was known that he had somehow gained control of the area's crime. Every robbery, every drug transaction, every prostitute, fell ultimately under his direction. He caused otherwise friendly murderers to fight among themselves, shoot, miss, and kill innocent bystanders. Dancers pulled their muscles. Hats would not fit on old men who had worn them for thirty years. Honest citizens would suddenly kick a police officer, and when brought to trial full of regret and shame, find themselves able to speak only Japanese.

Something was wrong in Ha Tikva. It became the topic of conversation at all the tables and in all the cafés. A man suggested to his friends that the strange things which happened were only a concealment and distraction in the case of the stranger who had arrived and done so well so suddenly. "You know, you may have a point there," said one of them just before the house collapsed, from termites said the newspaper, even though the house was made of stone.

The stranger was not to be seen, except on Friday nights, when a uniformed Cossack drove him through the streets in a lacquered red car. They invariably stopped in front of the house of Najime the Persian, the old sawyer, where the stranger sat from eight-thirty to nine-fifteen turning his feet to the front and then to the back again and again, and laughing a very ugly laugh that made children run to their mothers and rats race into their darkest tunnels—only to crash headlong against one another.

Najime stood slightly bent in back of the closed wood louvres, looking calmly at big brother from the mountain pass of a quarter of a century before. Yacov begged to be allowed to shoot him. "That is not the way," said Najime, "either the gun would explode, or you would miss and kill a friend. You see, he has undoubtedly grown in powers, but so have I. Like you, I probably would have wanted just to go and shoot him, and maybe then, when he and I were younger, I would have had a fair chance. But a young man is no match for him now. Look at all he has done and can do. He can kill effortlessly, but he must kill me as he said he would because I would not fear otherwise. And because he must kill me that way, he will not allow himself to be killed beforehand. So put your gun away. Either he will come here, or I will go to him. But I must think about this, because if I am right he has become so skillful in evil that we may even be dealing with the Devil himself. Anyway, this is beyond you, Yacov, because it calls for the strength of the past, the power of memory, the resolve of an old man's history, and because you are stupid.

"I have one advantage. I am not afraid. I must beat him down if only for the sake of the people of Ha Tikva. Even if I lose he may leave of his own will, but there is no guarantee. Now let me think about it, as if I were trying to find a way to move a large timber through a small door of a little house. Let me think for a while."

Najime walked every day to the seaside, and stayed there from noon to evening, smoking his pipe and staring at the white foam of the waves and their curling, like his smoke. He knew that an idea of victory could come either deliberately or on the air. But he knew also that ideas of victory which seem to travel on the air alight always on the shoulders of those who have been laboring in thought.

So for a week he left every day, descending the

stairs and walking across crowded boulevards, past great white ruins in the old part of the city, which was being leveled and cleared. But one morning as he and Yacov both were shaving in front of a copper bowl filled with boiling water, he clenched his fist around the razor, lifted his eyes, and said, "Aha! I did it once, and now I'll do it again!" He began to dance around the room, singing, jumping, and prancing, because he had solved his problem.

"Wonderful!" said Yacov. "What are you going to do?"

"Shut up!"

"Why shut up? I'm your son. Tell me."

"Shut up. I'll tell you, assuming that I'm alive, by tomorrow night."

The next morning, Najime arose and put on his best clothes. It was the day before a holiday and many people were dressed for the occasion even then. He wore an old double-breasted pin stripe suit, the stripes hardly visible, the cloth rough, deep, and blue. On his head he carried a Greek straw hat with a chocolate brown band, and in his belt under the coat was the knife he had brought from Persia. The handle was of leather washers, unusual for such a good knife since it deserved an ornamental grip. But in commissioning it Najime had not wanted that. The finest quality leather had become smooth and black over the years from the oil of his hand. A heavy nickel guard, curved inward, made it seem like a small sword. The blade itself was about a foot long, double edged only a few inches back from the tip in a fluted curve. It was cast from the best Swedish steel, which the smith had purchased from a Russian. Najime had sharpened it over the years, and especially carefully the night before. He had spent a good deal of his life sharpening blades. The knife was so sharp that he feared for the scabbard.

"Goodbye Yacov my son. I am going to the synagogue, and then to the barber." He winked.

Najime left and crossed the street, nodding and greeting as was his custom; alert as a young man hunting in the mountains he stood and prayed by the side of the road, since they were cleaning the synagogue. "Dear God, help me to know evil and to fight it. Help me to resist it, not that I would be evil myself, but that one of its principal parts is to appear as right and proper. And that is something I have wanted to discuss for a long time, but later. I am going, I believe, to do what you would have me do. Although I have not heard from you about this it seems the right thing to do."

He came to the street of the barber shop and walked toward it, adjusting his knife. Once inside he went directly to one of the old chairs and sat down, asking for a shave. The barber, a little Moroccan, began to lather Najime's face, already as cleanly shaven as a man's face could be. Najime had taken pains to do that just an hour before. The barber's manner was casual but somehow very mechanical and automatic, as if he were teaching young barbers. He then went to the razor drawer, picked out a very large razor with a transparent ice-blue handle, and began to sharpen it.

Within the white cloth Najime drew his knife, and as the barber approached with a look of boredom and sleep, Najime jumped from the chair, teeth exposed, the two sides of his mustache raised, and with a tremendously loud cry (the kind that used to go from one mountaintop to another), he stabbed the barber deep in his heart, pushing the knife right up to the hilt.

The other barbers and customers froze while their co-worker and barber of many years staggered in a half-circle, and then fell face down on the floor. Najime dropped back into the chair, feeling like a man who has just beaten the Devil. While the police were summoned, a soldier who had witnessed the incident through the window entered the shop and pompously trained his rifle on Najime, who had an angelic look.

The police came. They handcuffed Najime to the chair, and began to write in their books the statements of all concerned. The barbers stated that this man had come to their shop and killed Amzaleg, who was a third owner. They then described the killing in great detail, gesticulating, and glancing now and then at the body for fear of offending it with the color of their portraiture. Najime was silently shaking his head no. To everyone in the shop (by that time about 350 people, various animals, hawkers and vendors of every description, prostitutes plying their trade, entertainers, musicians, etc., etc.), he looked like a madman from an entirely different civilization.

A policeman turned to him and said, "What do you mean, shaking your head no like that?"

Najime replied, "That man is not their friend Amzaleg. Amzaleg is probably in bed with stomach trouble." The two remaining barbers looked at one another, confirming the presence of a madman. "He,"

continued Najime, "is an old enemy of mine from
Persia who swore to kill me with a razor, and that
was what he was about to do."

"Nonsense!" screamed the two remaining barbers
like twins. "That is Amzaleg, our friend and part-
ner."

"Turn him over," said Najime, hardly able to wait
until it was done. And when it was done, the long,
flat, half-bearded chin was not that of Amzaleg the
Moroccan barber, but of the big brother on the
mountain.

"Incredible," said the two barbers in unison.

Later, after he had been released by the police,
Najime went home under what seemed to be lighter
and cooler skies. Ha Tikva was awakening from a
week of hard work and about to await the sunset and
fine food of the holiday. It felt as though there were
going to be a rainstorm, although there was not going
to be one. Yacov was inside, having heard out the
window of all the strange events in the barber shop.
When his father came in and took off his coat, the son
was reverentially silent. But seeing that the older
man was in a good frame of mind, to say the least,
he cautiously asked, "How did you know he was the
barber?"

"Well," said Najime, "as a precautionary measure
I shaved this morning as cleanly as I could, and that
seemed to make no difference to this 'barber.' But
that was just a precaution, for any barber might have
been tired, and overlooked it."

"Then how did you know he would be there?"

"I didn't know for sure, but I took a chance. You
see, he vowed to kill me with a razor, and I have

never been to a barber in my life. Therefore, if I went
to a barber, it would have to be him. That is Devil's
conduct, and I have encountered it before. My suspi-
cion was confirmed when I noticed that he had no
wedding ring. Every barber in Israel wears a wedding ring. And then, I could feel his presence the way
sheep in mountains can feel the approach of a hunter. I have spent a lifetime waiting. I have won."

And both father and son heard the bakers scream-
ing, "It rises! It rises!" about their newly baked bread.
For during the previous few weeks the bread in Ha
Tikva Quarter had not risen. Najime was left to
spend the rest of his life pondering on whether he
had beaten the Devil or just the Devil's son, and
thinking about the clear air of his mountains and the
championships he had been born to take in sawing,
chopping, and many village games.

Because of the Waters of the Flood

Jets from airfields in Nevada trailed fine white lines across the sky. At the head of white columns the planes themselves looked like silver ticks. When she looked up, there was a roundness of light as if she were seeing through glass or a lens, but she was only looking through her eyes. All her life the B-52's had left their smoke trails above her. It was almost a part of nature, akin to the rising of the moon, or setting of the sun.

They were miles from Tippet, a town of about thirty-five, and Tippet was miles from anywhere else. You could pull in two or three country music stations. Sheep grazed in the lower depressions of the mountains and drank from clear pools, near gray porous rocks. In summer Henry made a fire, and lining his sheep up one by one he pulled off the ticks and cast them into the flame. Always the air was cool and deep. Around the house was no argument, no lawn—just pine trees, wind, and a view of mountains. Winter was hard and sometimes it snowed late in June, though only at night. They were high up where the air was thin. They didn't waste it. Stories were therefore short, expressions clipped, and Agnes had a habit of giving long looks without saying a word, during which her mouth was slightly smiling and her eyebrows slightly raised. When she looked this way, everyone knew she was good-natured and wanted to kiss her and twirl, eyes closed, with so much in reserve.

She cooked. Steam swirled upward around the spoon as she looked into the pot, her body arched away from the stove. The kitchen was full of windows. Through them was miraculous blue and white of mountains, hanging aerial ice, and sky.

And her face. Her face was an extremely beautiful face. When she laughed you did not laugh at her face nor did she become less pretty. When she was angry it was the same. The eyes were blue. There was a mirror in the hall, surrounded by a frame of grayish-white tin. When she looked at herself in the mirror she saw the blue eyes, shining out, and the simple blond hair, energetic. "Bong Bong," she said as she patted her hair into place and went to the porch to wait for Henry.

She was wearing a loose white dress held together at the neck by a button which said, "All the Way with Alf Landon." The wind blew her hair. She settled her eyes to stare into the valley, past the rocks, past the sheep that looked like moving cylinders of cream or cloud, past the pools and pines, to the road where Henry would be coming. She picked up a knife and stuck it into the chopping block on which it had been lying. She loved Henry, and had doused everything to marry him. Those are the only marriages that work—where you say to hell with it, and hurt three or four dozen people, and tell fifty more to go to hell, and then move out to Nevada or Alaska, or Brazil. If you don't do that, you're not really married. She was married to Henry. Henry tried to tell their parents about how to marry.

"Why?" said their parents.

"Because," said Henry, "if you love you make no concessions—none at all. And in the beginning this is especially true. And Agnes and I are angry at concessions—little ones, big ones. We want to start clean. I love Agnes. We bought a sheep ranch."

The pot was boiling over. She went in and turned off the heat. It was a simple principle: if the pot boils over, turn off the heat. She always thought passionately that to think is somehow dispassionate. Henry said she was right and drove her in his car up the mountain to their house with the whitening tin-framed mirror where they saw themselves in dusty silver and wondered what was the toughest road they knew.

She went back to her chair on the porch. She led an orchestra with the spoon, and sang several songs. Henry was a hard worker, very strong for his size, and he made up stories. He never went anywhere without adventures. He once had wept in her lap at the top of a mountain. She kissed her hands, ran them down her breast, and said a prayer, for she believed in God, as did Henry—in His power, and that He made everything. That is really why they told everyone to go to hell, for they needed no one, and saw that no one believed.

She prayed to God, surveying His hills and rising high above them, glancing at green pines, and turning humorous circles in heaven. She loved God, and she loved Henry. God made her shake like a true priest, and although she was quiet she was thundering at the hills for His sake, and for Henry's sake.

Henry came up the mountain in the wooden station wagon. There were books on the seat next to him, and groceries in the back. He was driving to music. She could see by the way he moved his head from side to side and was rhythmically intent on making the car sway gracefully up and down turns, through the cool sunshine air.

He pulled up and left the radio on. He got out of the car and walked around the front to face Agnes, who was on the porch as still as a branch.

He was dark-haired and had a wide smile. He wore a bulky olive Navy N-1 jacket, denim pants, and brown leather boots. She looked at him and remembered what she had looked like in the mirror—tan, her nose a little shiny, in a white dress and crown of blond, with blue eyes sadly piercing the leaded glass darkened from age in the mountains.

They were still, and the wind ceased. "Well," she said, and raised her eyebrows slightly.

"I told them that I wouldn't go," he said. "That I wouldn't go to prison either, that we both would go into the mountains and fight there to the death, on the little point, for what we believed. And when I said it, I meant it. We're right, aren't we, Agnes?"

"Yes."

"Then they met for about ten minutes. When they came out, the psychiatrist took me aside and told me I was not fit for military service."

Agnes lifted the sheets of her dress, floated down the steps, twirled in slow motion over millions of particles of white dust, circled dizzy around Henry while he laughed and leaned back and looked at her blue sparkling eyes. "We're both crazy," he said. "Aren't we?"

"Yes," said Agnes, "and we're free." And they sat on the wooden steps of the porch and said that the day was especially fine.

"Why," Henry said, "do you have that spoon so tightly in your hands?"

And Agnes began to cry.

Ruin

My father was a cattle rancher in Jamaica. One day after the war he had become sick after eating a bad piece of frozen meat, and that was it. Suddenly all our cane went down and men began putting up fences. By himself my father took the Oracabessa launch to Cuba, went up into the mountains he said, and came back a week later with a Cuban he had known during the war in North Africa. Pappy was his name, and he had two teeth in his mouth and looked thin and stupid, but knew cattle.

It was a risk for my father to take the Oracabessa launch across the straits in September. It was only ninety miles, but September in Jamaica is the time for bad storms; they come up quickly. He was very daring, my mother told me, after the war, and I remember it a bit myself. All the men were a little like that. My mother said that after Al Alamain my father thought he could do anything. He was impetuous,

like a young boy, the war having taught him both
how temporary life is, and how valuable.

He had been a cane grower all his life, that was
what he knew, but he was willing to learn cattle. He
put every penny, every quattie of what we had, into
a small herd, and a prize black bull that came from
Corpus Christi in October and was lowered from the
freighter to the dock, hung from a bright yellow
sling. When the yellow sash was dropped away and
we could see the bull's blackness and the rotations
of green that were its eyes, my father was a proud
man. The bull looked up and snorted, its eyes fixed
on the mountain, and Pappy said with a hideous gentle smile that it smelled the herd, and that the sea
voyage had done it no good.

Our house had red tiles on the roof. They glowed
vermilion in the sun. We heard drums on Friday and
Saturday nights; drifting up from the town, the sound
was marvelous and frightening. When my father was
troubled he walked down the mountain on the winding road, and stayed for a long time on the wall overlooking the sea. It was terribly hot and still in the
morning. Everyone wore white. I was often aware
of carrion rotting unseen in some soft place.

I was quite surprised when, a week after we took
the bull off the ship, Pappy ran onto the terrace and
turning his straw hat rapidly in his hands announced
that the bull had gone wild and was killing the other
animals. My father got up slowly and put down the
Gleaner. He was in white pants and a white shirt, and
he was stained beautifully with colors, for he had
been painting a picture; he had been painting fish
and fruit. I followed him to his room where I watched

him load a .30-06, pushing in the dull brass cartridges one by one. He seemed to be angry and perhaps a little frightened. I was frightened for him.

We started at a walk down the hill but then we began to run. At the bend Hamid was waiting for us with two horses, a beautiful black one for my father and the nice brown one called Kerry for Pappy. My father pulled me up behind him and we flew down the hill with the Trades whipping our hair and flinging Pappy's hat onto his back where it hung by a cord. The rifle bumped against my face and I had trouble hanging on but we reached the field, which was streaked with the blood of cows as if some Japanese had been flying kites with long red ribbons which when the wind died were left parallel on the grass. The blood steamed, especially near the places where cows had fallen. Some of them groaned but most were just breathing deeply as if they hoped to get better.

The bull was at the end of the field and his head was covered and clotted with blood; it made thick cakes which clung to his hair. He was stained with red.

My father told me to hang on tightly, and I made my thin arms a tourniquet around his waist. I was very much afraid of falling off the horse. I could smell the paint on my father's shirt and the sun made me blink. He put the rifle in a sling position, so he could hold it in one hand and the reins in another. He did it quickly and well; it must have been one of the things he learned in North Africa. He spurred the horse and it started to prance, foaming, toward the bull. Silent Jamaicans pressed against the fences. They were watching us on the wet black horse.

The horse danced sideways at the bull, elegantly, as if we were not in a green palm ring on a cliff above the sea but in a London riding academy.

The bull stomped the ground. My father cocked the rifle. The horse, rocking and edging, had spasms of fright. That black horse was a good horse. He was frightened but he risked his life for what as far as he knew was my father's whim. My father said that if he could be as good a man as that horse was a horse, he would be happy and ready to rest. Pappy called the black horse an astronomer, because at night he looked long into the air at the stars, sometimes for hours.

The bull charged us and I felt my father's muscles tense as he aimed quickly and fired. I did not see the bull fall because I had turned my head away. But I saw the waves of our action in the faces of the people at the fences, who started, and then cheered. As we trotted away from the bull's body I looked back. There were two large red holes in the neck. I had remembered only one shot.

We visited the cows one by one and killed them. The horse seemed more frightened of them than of the bull. My father said, "Now we are going to have to get rid of all this meat, and buy new cows dammit."

"New ones?" I said. He did not answer. "Can we . . . ?" I did not finish.

We went up the hill at a walk. It was hot, and the hooves of the black horse were scarlet.

First Russian Summer

His hand shaking, fingers spread so that the old man was imploring with the very breadth of his grasp for the attendant to be silent, he made the room still. The curtains ceased billowing inwards, and a reddish light from afternoon and the bricks seemed to dim. The difference between an old man and a boy is so great that in explaining himself, assuming that he can, an old man will want much time and silence. In order to give time and silence one must have great respect, perhaps the reason the young are taught to defer, not for the sake of deference itself, but to give them an opportunity to learn lessons of difficulty. Of course there are old fools, but when guiding young fools their experience can be invaluable. If a man, even an average man, has learned well by observation, then he should be in great demand. One might think young men could easily consider their fathers and grandfathers a most precious resource, aside from allowance and inheritance. Since it is not that way and wisdom finds no market, old men spend much time talking to white walls.

This old man, though he lived in the Hebrew Home for the Aged, was not the kind of fellow to spend all morning putting on his pants. He was aged it is true, and he had no one, no one, and nothing, that is true too. But age was something inappropriate to him, having come by accident in between observations of great magnitude. He looked quite unlike the other patients in that he was tan and ruddy. His strong face and gleaming eyes showed that he spent many hours in the sun, if only in the garden, and that here was a man who although heavy with age was as light inside as a man could be, a man whose imagination and memories kept him in steady forward flight and beat down time as easily as white gulls rise high on currents of shimmering blue air.

At eighty he found himself able to make a powerful case for that which he thought just and good, and like all good men he found himself most of the time alone in a world which insists on the worship of local gods, a world blind to the fact of its own creation, being, and turning, a world of clever bugs who have a buggish strut and who make excuses for their mortality in the minute and insignificant gas of their works. The greatness of the world he thought is not in anything man has done but in what God has done. And this made him remember a time long ago. It was a simple memory, but he loved it, and in recalling it he felt the color of his life.

As a little boy he had gone for the summer to his grandfather's timber forests. That was in 1884, and

his little boy's face and eyes were to see the whole
world shudder and break and become alive again
more than once. But then he was just a child who had
seen nothing, more than thirty years before the October Revolution, in the Russia of Czar Nicholas,
when he remembered the world to be vastly green
and young, with so many colors just beyond his sight,
and he had for a little boy such a grown-up sense of
the beauty of the world. It impressed him deeply
then with the simplest it had to offer, lessons taken
early from no man but from his first views, which in
all their power saw him through the shaking of history and into his age.

His grandfather met him at the station. It seemed
as if the train had taken a lifetime for it had gone
more than a thousand miles from Odessa. And a small
sleepy blond boy with large brown eyes and a minia-
ture suit and suitcase had rushed into his grandfather's arms in tears, since he had never been fully
convinced that the train was not an eternal matter
and he himself doomed to live the rest of his life in
various forms of rolling stock. But his grandfather
had met him in a small black carriage pulled by a
spotted horse with a white mane. The fresh air was
good for the child as he watched the horse watching
the road they traveled.

When they reached a high ridge overlooking a
stand of timber, fir and pine as far as the eye could
see, his grandfather stopped the carriage and they
both looked out on the light and dark green. Sunlight
was golden and the air at that altitude was cool and
clear. They were alone in vastness. "Levi," his grandfather said, "this is the finest thing on earth, these

trees and mountains, not because I own them because I don't, as my land is not visible from here, and besides, no man owns the land. Those are man's games. This is the finest thing on the earth, not any painting or books or music, but these trees."

"Why, Grandpa?" said Levi, who was already convinced.

"Because, Levi, God made the forest and this clear air. And even if there were a man who couldn't see that, he could see the shape of things and how astonishing they are." Then he gave the horse its rein and took the little boy through twenty miles of trees, a forest which would turn even a vain actress away from herself. Levi learned that soft lesson and it became the steel of his life. Whenever he wanted he could put himself on that road, wide-eyed in the cool air, rushing through a newborn greenness in a time when the world loved its open spaces and colors signified all there was to know. The little boy was still in the man, as the man had been in the little boy that day when all time touched the depth of a young child in his grandfather's timber forests.

Katrina, Katrin'

It had been a terrible Christmas. Two young men stood in the dark on a subway platform. A small orange line was at the bottom of the sky, and the stars were bright white in the blue just above the horizon. Directly overhead the sky was black, so a man's eyes were caught and dazzled by a great mass of constellations in the cold January wind. New snow from that morning made everything quiet, and the two men, who were almost young enough to be called boys, stood in a small drift at the platform's end. They were looking into blackness which seemed to move with the wind. Their cheeks were red and flushed. They were dressed nearly alike, for both were clerks and both worked behind yellow wooden desks with green glass-vizored lamps. They were paid exactly eighty-six dollars and fifty cents a week and they banked at the same bank. To the middle-aged women in the office and to the executives the only difference between the two was that one had a mustache, a short black mustache, very dapper, and the other did not. And they had different weeks each year for vacations, one in August, one in June, and they had, of course, different names, although they were often called by the wrong one.

"I think," said the one without the mustache, "that I'm going to get married. You know, to that girl I told you about, Ruth, whose father is a lawyer. You know, Ruth. I told you about her. She's the one I took to Philadelphia, the one who is very funny."

"Oh yes," said the other man, "the one who is very funny. Did you ask her?"

"No. I haven't really decided yet. It's a big step, a very big step. I'll have to spend the rest of my life with her, and unless I go cavorting around that means she will be the only woman I will sleep with from now until forever—and I love her so I don't plan to go cavorting around."

"Well if you really love her, then marry her."

"I just don't know."

"If you don't know, then you don't really love her."

"I do love her. I'm crazy about her."

"Then you should have no doubts. If she's the one, really the one, you should know it."

"Look, Biferman, I don't see anything wrong with having some doubt before such a tremendous transaction. It's normal. Why not? And anyway, you never went out with a girl in your life. How would you know?"

"I went out with a girl."

"What, in high school? I'll bet you did. You forget,

Biferman. There are no girls in DeWitt Clinton. I went there too."

"You didn't know me then," Biferman said angrily, looking more intently at the darkness.

"Do I really need to have known you then? I know you now. I see you on Sunday walking alone in Van Cortlandt Park. I spend forty hours a week within two feet of you. I go home on the same train. I meet you in the morning, rain or shine, on the corner. What is there you have hidden from me, Biferman, what is it that gives you the right to tell me, when finally after so many years of being alone I find someone I think I can love, that I don't really love her? For Christ's sake what am I supposed to do, be a perfectionist? I can't do that. I just can't do it. I can't stand being alone. It'll work out. Biferman, I can't stand being alone."

"*I* can stand being alone," said Biferman.

"Well then, maybe you're unhuman. Maybe you'll spend the rest of your life at that desk and go home every night in the cold to a dark room, and eat every night at Katz's, and what the hell do you do in the evening anyway?"

"I thought you knew me."

"Oh, now I know. You're going to give me a story about a woman you keep."

"Nothing like that at all."

"You don't keep a woman?"

"No."

"You had a girl then?"

"Yes, I had a girl. I don't want to talk about it."

"No, tell me. Please, I want to know."

"Look you. I don't know what you think or how

you think, but if you're thinking that being within two feet of me for forty hours a week gives you a good idea of what I'm like, well then I wouldn't even tell you how much I earn each week."

"Eighty-six fifty, shmuck. And by the way I'm your only friend."

"I guess you are my only friend."

"Yeah. And you know something else, it's difficult to say, but you're my only friend too."

The train came. They boarded without a word and since Biferman could never in the world have shouted what he so badly wanted to say, since Biferman could never in the world have shouted under any circumstance, he was silent during the ride, and he just looked off the track at the sparkling lights on dark bridges, and the little red lights of planes in the sky moving toward Queens and the airports, the flashing of car headlamps, a faraway neon which seemed so much like a jewel in velvet, the thin black trees, and the wind which in some moments he was sure he could see.

At the end of the line, where the subway stops in an orange-roofed building above the street near Van Cortlandt Park, they exited by the appropriate stairs and when they reached the street, cut across an enormous field which seemed like prairie country, or even the steppes of Central Asia in winter, for it was dark and the wind whipped the fine snow in their faces as they walked with heads bent to the stars which might have been the stars of the clear desert or the stars of the sea so bright and beautiful were they, and as they walked they gained confidence for they were away from the city, undefeated, free.

"Harold. When I was in high school I was fond of reading. I still am. As soon as I did not have to go to Hebrew School anymore I had time to read. Do you know the bookstore on 231 Street near Broadway?"

"Of course, I pass it all the time. The one with novels and history mainly. Rosen's?"

"Yes, Rosen's."

"What about it."

"Well . . . well . . . do you know Mr. Rosen?"

"I don't know him, but I assumed it was a Mr. Rosen who owns the store. After all, it is called Rosen's Bookstore."

"It is called, 'Rosen, dash, Books,' as in Russia."

"Go on."

"God it's so cold. It's so cold now."

"Go on, Biferman."

"Rosen had a daughter. Her name was Katrina, or Katrin'. Katrina Rosen. She was born in Russia. They didn't come until after the war. Rosen lost his wife in a camp. He is a broken man. He is my friend. I forgot to say that. He *is* my friend. I was in high school and I used to go when school let out and buy a book at Rosen's. I read a book every night. Of course I took from the library, but I would buy a book each week from Rosen and it usually took me about two or three hours in the store to decide which to buy. Rosen's daughter, Katrina, worked in the store. She sat on a high stool behind a desk and catalogued books on white cards she put in a file. I was eighteen.

"She was seventeen. And she was a most beautiful, delicate girl. She had red hair which fell to her waist, and the finest white skin, and such beautiful eyes. She was always so delicate, and when I came into the

store she turned very red and stared excessively at
her cards, making deft meaningless motions with her
pen. I pursed my lips when I looked at a book, acting
serious and scholarly. I don't know how I did it for
two or three hours at a stretch. Half the time I was
interested in the book, the other half was just a game
since I thought only of her.

"For three or four months, all during the fall of my
senior year, I did not say a word to her, not a word.
If I wanted a book I couldn't reach or had to make
an inquiry I asked Rosen himself and he would drag
out his ladder or go to the card file, and it would be
done. I thought about her all the time. I knew her
name because I heard him call her Katrina. 'Katrina,'
he would say, 'have you written up the Poliakov book
yet?' or 'Katrin,' my dear, did *Baron's Social and Re-
ligious* come in yet?' and she always turned very red
because she knew I was listening and answered, 'Yes
Father, yes my dear father.'

"I walked in the park each Saturday, dressed as
nicely as I could manage, for miles, hoping I would
meet her in the afternoon. I never did. Everywhere
I went I thought I would come across her but I never
saw her outside the store.

"One day I went into Rosen's, and old Rosen had
a cold. He was not there. She ran the store. A carton
of Hebrew books had just come in. You know how
the old people still buy Hebrew books, and Yiddish.
Well Rosen usually handled the Hebrew books, but
he was sick, so she had to do it and her Hebrew was
atrocious—charming, but atrocious. I began my little
game of leafing, trying for the courage to speak to
her, until I noticed she was looking all the time in a

dictionary. I walked very quietly to the desk, and in
the yellow light saw all the books, and a few badly
written Hebrew index cards.

" 'Tov is with a tet' I said, and she looked up at me,
her face shining in the light.

" 'Do you know Hebrew well?' she said.

" 'Oh yes,' I said, 'very well.'

" 'I didn't think you were Jewish,' she said.

" 'I am,' I said.

" 'Will you help me?' she said.

" 'Yes,' I said.

" 'What is this then?' She pointed to an underlined
passage.

" 'Shir HaShirim,' I said, 'The Song of Songs.'

" 'Oh yes, I see it now.'

" 'Can you read it?' I asked.

" 'Not really.'

" 'Try this passage.'

" 'I can't,' she said, looking at me from very close.
We were right next to one another. I translated for
her. It was from dalet.

" 'Walk with me from Lebanon, from Lebanon
come. Look . . . from the peak of Shenir, and Her-
mon, from lions' dens, from mountains of the leopards. Thou hast ravished my heart, my sister, my
bride, with one of your eyes, with one chain from
your neck . . .'

"And then we were silent, and I looked in her eyes
for a long time.

"By the time I left my sleeves were up and I felt
entirely comfortable. We had catalogued and
shelved all the books shipped in that day. She said:
'I couldn't go to Hebrew school most times. I was

very sick when I was little,' and she turned red, so red, as if she were on fire when she said that. 'There's nothing to be ashamed of,' I said, 'I was not so healthy myself.'

"From then on I began to talk to her. I found I could talk to her better than to anyone. We understood one another perfectly. We went to the park in the evening. Right here, right in this spot, in the spring and in the summer, we walked past children playing and the kites were like confetti above us, and the sky was clear blue. We could hear shouts far away on the fields. Everyone was dressed in colorful clothes, and the smoke from apartment buildings was beautiful, curling against that new sky, that fresh sky, and the old people on the benches were a good sight to see. The old people here are such gentle people.

"When I was a freshman at City she was a senior at Music and Art. We went to school and came back together. I knew I would love her all my life. That is why I said what I said to you. Do you remember Peter Aaron? In his house there was a fireplace with gas jets so it was always steady and bright, like the best of wood fires. It never ran down. I loved Katrina just like that. Always bright, never still. Powerful always, never unsteady.

"But Katrina had been very sickly as a child. Perhaps that is why her skin was so white and fine and when she blushed she seemed to be the color of the deepest red velvet," said Biferman as he looked at the stars, thinking that one of the things he could have been was an astronomer, and they might have lived in a big house, and he could have taken her to

look at the moon which in an old-fashioned telescope, he knew, has a bright blue rim. And perhaps
as they looked at the moon with its bright blue rim
he would have kissed her thin lips and entangled her
long red hair in his hands, and held her very close
to him making her whiter than even her fine white
skin or the white of the moon, and feeling the delicacy of her, the delicacy of Katrina, Katrina Rosen,
the daughter of the bookstore man.

"She had been very sickly, Katrina. And when I
was a sophomore at City, majoring in History, she got
sick again, in November. In the beginning of November she became so deathly sick that her father prayed
all the time with tears in his eyes. He raged at God,
and shouted in the store, in the street. He was furious
at God. 'God. God. How dare you take from me my
wife, and make my daughter deathly sick. There is
no God,' and then he would weep and fall to his
knees near the couch, burying his head in the cush-
ion. 'There is no God,' he said, and then he said, 'God,
God, God, Lord of Israel, how can you do this?'

"I was young. I am not afraid to say that I enjoyed
it in a way. It gave me a chance to care for her, and
my love was so much grounded on care; don't all the
Jews love by caring? So as long as she could talk, and
read, and listen when I read to her, and learn the Hebrew I was teaching her, it was all right.

"But I cannot begin to describe the panic into
which I was hurled when she began to get worse.
Rosen knew from the start, but I was only nineteen.
He had seen enough in his life to tell him, but I
walked through the park, happy like an idiot. The
fields right here in the Bronx were so golden, so

bright, as if in a foreign place, that I was sure God would not forsake her. If I saw such beauty, how could He not do so? Neither of my parents had died. I had not yet seen a true winter.

"By Christmas Katrina was as white as the snow in the park and she spent most of the day with her eyes closed. She was wasting away and the doctors at Montefiore could do nothing but offer pompous opinions which were all wrong. Her father knew immediately. His wife was turned into potash for some green German field. How could they have fooled him? We sat in silence, Rosen and I, in a delicatessen below the elevated near Montefiore, wondering about the flower, Katrina, who was within the whiteness and sterility of that great smoking red-brick place of death and healing. And then she became red with a fever that never left her. They moved her at last to home. Rosen bought a cot and I lived there. We cared for her almost with a vengeance, day and night. For Rosen it was a vengeance. He was fighting God, a ridiculous little old man, fighting the murderous God of Israel. He had great energy, that old man; he could have made an empire. We all could have made an empire, couldn't we have, but we were always too busy fighting and loving God, the bastard, God, how I love him, and how I hate.

"I lived there, and while Rosen was at the store I cared for Katrina. I kissed her when she was sick, furiously. I know I shouldn't have, but I often approached the bed and kissed her, kissed her hot face and held her to me until she sighed and slept. She was weak but she gripped me with all the strength she had, all the strength of a delicate young girl of eighteen who was dying. When I kissed her I was saying to God, 'God don't you see how strong she was and how beautiful? Don't take her. Don't take her.'

"On the twelfth of January, Rosen was at the store and I was making tea for Katrina. At that time the doctor came four times a day. She was burning, I was making tea for Katrina and the gas stove was buckling and burning. She called me, in almost a whisper, and she said, 'Aryeh, Aryeh, do you know the lights that Christians have on their Christmas trees, the lights with a column of bubbling water? When you turn them on they bubble after a little while. Please get me some. I think if I see them I'll get better. I feel better, and I want to look at some light.'

"I became terribly excited. At last she is better, I thought. When I get the lights she will be better. I had faith in omens and I was sure that Katrina would not die, that the lights would be the things which would make her better and restore to her a natural color. It was the first time in months she had said she felt better. The lights I was sure could make her able to walk with me in the park, and catalogue her books at the store, and make love, and run about and laugh as she was so fond of doing. She was wild, Katrin', just wild the way she would jump around and scream and grab onto me and kiss me as if her life depended on it.

"I went all around Kingsbridge, looking for that type of Christmas light. I couldn't find it. The merchants said that all Christmas lights had been returned to the factory. 'There's no need for them,' one said. 'Of course there is,' I said. 'No there isn't. Nobody needs them. It's January twelfth and nobody needs Christmas lights.'

"So I went to the phone book and called Christmas Tree Light Companies. There are dozens in New York. Only one had a supply. They sent me to their warehouse, on Sedgwick Street in Brooklyn. Do you know where Sedgwick Street is? It's near the docks, in a tough neighborhood. I was not afraid to go there. I stood in front in the subway and urged it on like a jockey on a horse and I paid no attention to the cold wind. It just made my face red, and I rushed through Brooklyn running in the sleet to Sedgwick Street. It's a Puerto Rican section, and I smelled *arroz con pollo* from the little restaurants. I went right to the warehouse, near the harbor, which is the sea. The sleet fell into the sea and the sea swayed up against the gray stone wall and sprayed the street, and I entered the place. It was lit by a few naked bulbs.

"A little bald man was yelling at five or six blacks. He was fierce. He cursed them. He abused them. He called them names and gave them precise instructions.

"I ran up to him and took him by the shoulders. He smelled of oil, or perhaps it was from the sea, or a truck fueling outside. I said, 'My wife is dying. Give me Christmas tree lights, the kind that bubble, and maybe she will be better.'

"He thought I was crazy. He thought I was a madman, especially since I was red and soaking wet and trembling all over. 'Christmas tree lights?' he said. 'All right, how many?' 'Just one set,' I said, 'one set. Please hurry.'

"He gave me a strange look and then called his

men together. 'You see this boy,' he said, 'his wife is dying, so he needs the kind of lights that bubble, model three, you know, who's gonna get them for him?' They laughed. The whole warehouse was steaming, cold, and dark. Shreds of red packing on the floor made the place look like a battlefield where many men had been slaughtered. The oil smoke was choking. Someone must have been clearing a chimney nearby. One finally spoke. 'I'll get them,' he said, 'I know where they are.' He was a thin black man. He looked like he was dying himself, from the labor, from the cold, and he ran to a freight elevator. In a minute he was back, smiling and graceful as he ran. He gave me the lights. He said, 'Take off man.' The bald-headed man said, "Wait, don't you believe in paying?' But the other man said, 'Take off!' and threw his arm violently outward, toward the door. 'You don't got time, go!' and I left, running."

Biferman and Harold reached the edge of the park where Biferman was to go one way and Harold the other. They stood in the field still under the stars which in the clear air of blackest night were violent in their cool sparkling. Biferman went on, in the cold wind, as red as he had been in the sleet of that January.

"It took me so long to get home, but when I did I ran all the way from the subway to the Rosens'. I was planning a party. When we were engaged she had worn a dress of black velvet, and when we drank champagne I took her into the hall and we stood by the tricycles, kissing. A little boy came out of another apartment and gasped. Katrin' laughed although she was concerned that he was so worried.

"I was planning as I ran, a get-well party, even though I had always been afraid of parties. It would be so joyous—to have such a party.

"Rosen was not yet home from the store. I unpacked the lights and tiptoed into Katrina's room. It was so quiet. I could hear the wind outside but I did not notice the sound of her breathing. I had already plugged in the lights when I realized she was not breathing. I clipped them to a white curtain, one by one, until they were strung out gaily in a chain. There were about twenty of them, a deluxe set. I knew she was not breathing. My plan was to let the lights warm up and start to bubble before I awakened her. I could not hear her breathing, but I pretended that I could, for a long time, until the lights were warm. And when they started to bubble and they cast a beautiful warm light and I could feel the heat from them, a red glow on my face, I said through my tears, 'Katrina . . .' and she did not answer, 'Katrina,' I said, 'Katrina my love . . . Katrin'? . . . I brought you the lights.' She did not answer."

Biferman looked up, his eyes closed, and said quietly, "Thou hast ravished my heart, my sister, my bride."

Shooting the Bar—1904

Michael had been to London, and Paris too. Suzanna had no solid idea of what these places were like. Casco Bay had surrounded every instant of her life with its mists or its waves, or its storms that brought the angry Atlantic almost to the door of her house, which she locked at night if Michael were still out at sea. Suzanna had the most beautiful face in all of Maine, perhaps in all the world. It was a clear face which seemed to make its own light; its features were light and did not seem to depend on each other. When Michael first saw her he imagined she might be easily capable of walking through walls, so fresh and energetic was her manner. "She is sunlight," he said.

She loved the Bible, "because it is beautiful," she said, and she read it every morning. She dreamed of the places Michael had been, imagining herself a captain's wife, or perhaps a contemporary princess of

Russia, one whose life went from peak to peak, oper-
atically encountering dozens of carpeted stairs lined
with mirrors as she ran to the high heat and noise of
a ballroom. How many times had she been carried
by imagination from the beach to an open carriage.
The horses were white and perfectly clean, the path
straight and arched by French trees. Musicians were
everywhere in the park, playing Brahms by bronze
fountains that splashed in the day and would splash
in the dark. Bright colored leopards and lions in zoos
paced gracefully in front of her, and by her side was
Michael with his strong face, somehow as a European, dressed and looking as if an artist had painted
him, which was how she thought all Europeans were.

Suzanna was Mrs. Ashley, something that for the
several years of its existence had never ceased to surprise her. She wondered if she ever would or could
feel like her mother, who was purely Mrs. Tyler, and
seemed to have been always the wife of Suzanna's
father, Suzanna's mother, and the mother of Suzanna's brothers. At church when Tom had come back
from whaling and said, "Suzanna Tyler," Michael
said with great authority and delight, *"Suzanna Ashley,"* and Tom, who had always been in love with
her, turned very red and rotated back in his pew.
The preacher preached to all the brown eyes focused
on him like a diagram in optics. If the eyes had had
half Suzanna's radiance the preacher would have
burned. She had always been special and strange.

Michael was once a thin boy who wore
gold-rimmed glasses and loved books. He was best
with boats, always managed to catch more fish than
could his friends, and he spent so much time in the

dunes and the pines reading or walking or feeling
October, that when he came into town it was as if
he had come back from the sea. People asked him
questions, and he told them stories full of lies that
were true.

After graduation Suzanna had become a teacher
of little children, and Michael had gone into the
navy, for he changed. He began to hate Three Mile
Harbor, and he brooded all day in the woods or at
work lifting heavy barrels at the wharf. As his face
began to take shape and become less boyish, he
wished for new scenery and a place to answer or
drown his questions, so he left on a frigate from Port-
land, and went around the world. In his youth he
touched the shores of Egypt and Arabia, marched
into Peking, tried to fake familiarity on his first trip
to Paris, loved Rome, spent more hours than re-
quired on his watch straddling the bowsprit looking
at the Wedgwood-colored clouds and sky.

After a year he began to think of Suzanna, and
found that he could not stop thinking about her, nor
did he want to. Every city, every stretch of sea, every
special storm, strange sailor, oddly draped dwarf,
beautiful bridge, or full and luxuriant tropical tree
he saw, was captured in his mind as a present for her.
He talked to her on lookout as the ship pitched in a
gray sea. He closed his eyes and kissed her as the
spray wet the forecastle. His greatest fear was that
when he came home she would be taken.

He kept a journal, and despite the fact of his delin-
quency, "March 21, 1900 . . . December 22, 1900,"
wrote some good things. He wanted to tell her about
the beaches of Alexandria, "which are bordered by

poppies and sea-lakes, and clean, bright, white, blue, and washed by the winds of Africa from the west. Thousands of years of man cannot spoil even the thin rim of this place"; of Athens and the Acropolis, "Yesterday I was at the Acropolis, and although it is very beautiful and affords a beautiful view, I was much disappointed. They are only buildings, and stone, and stone is akin to dust which is everywhere and too much. I am done with antiquities, suspicious of dreams; Suzanna is my only relevance."

Late on a winter night when the snow quieted Three Mile Harbor and put out the street lights, when it edged beautifully on the merchant's tin and wooden signs, when it hissed into chimneys, Michael came dressed in black (with a broader face than he had had when he left) to the store and sail loft, where they hardly recognized him. Tom strained in the yellow gas light. "Michael?" Michael had an important question. Then he ran through the snow all the miles to Suzanna's house, where much out of breath he came into a warm room. There were two bright fires, and they burned strongly, heating the air until Suzanna's cheeks were vermilion, as were Michael's from the touch of the snow. Her parents bustled about and gently maneuvered Michael into a chair. The gas lamps were yellow and singing, the window black and frosted, and Suzanna's eyes were blasting back at Michael the heat of a forge. They looked directly at each other.

He saw that things were not the same, but better, that she was a woman and better than a girl, and then for the first time, before they had said a word, he realized that he had changed and become a man. With-

out once consulting his journal, Michael told Suzanna
all that had happened to him, and evidently he told
it well. They were married.

When the President arose that day and glanced at
the sky through a window in the White House, he
sent for his favorite artist, and told him to duplicate
the blue of the sky on all the medals, banners, and
plumes of the army and the navy. The artist said
quite flatly that it was impossible.

Suzanna Tyler Ashley stood by a wooden table
next to their water pump. She was wearing a new
white linen apron, starched, dazzling, and large, and
she was opening clams, buckets of them. An autumn
day without a cloud, the wind and the sea were
fierce. After cutting the mud-colored back muscle
she pushed the knife into the shell and worked it
around until the two halves separated and her pink
fingers were wet. She put the meat in a bowl and the
juice in a bottle. Occasionally she would drink from
a particularly well formed shell, holding it to her lips,
bending her eyes to see the absolute white pearly
cup; the wind was so wild it made little waves and
bubbles in the liquid before she drank it. It washed
in the shell like a small sea, and the shell was the color
of her apron which was the color of the clouds and
the whitecaps on the sea, which was blue like the sky
and her eyes. She felt in her dreaming a power; she
felt as if she were conjuring the wind.

Several months past when they were traveling to
Boston they had argued on the way. Michael in a rage
stopped the horses, tied the reins, and jumped off the
wagon, leaving it and her by the side of the road. She

looked straight ahead and pridefully refused to
watch him or turn. A group of sailors came down the
road, crowded into a wagon, drunk, rowdy. As they
neared she wanted to run to Michael, for they had
seen her golden hair from afar and all eyes were centered upon her. As a compromise, she took out a mirror and moved it until she saw the comforting image
of Michael leaning against a tree, looking with great
wisdom at the group of sailors (for he was an alumnus
of their life and older) and with great love at her, for
he loved what she had done with the mirror.

Michael was getting lobsters from his traps; doing
it made him feel like a sorcerer. She could see him
in the tiny green boat with the white sail he raised
when he moved from float to float. Had he known
the wind would rise as it had he would not have gone
out, for the fishermen of Three Mile Harbor were
like lobsters who are clever enough to get out of the
coil; they had to shoot between two sides of a jetty
over a bar, and negotiate a thin channel funnel.
There had been deaths there.

Suzanna felt as if she, and he, and the century itself, were on the verge of a discovery. She dreamed
always of the remote and thought it one reason why
Michael loved her so. Beneath her white and gold
New England face were thoughts that went deep
into the tropics and skirted jungles full of richer,
darker colors, colors of fast and intense life. This
woman sat in church and, taking the rhythm from
the organ, put herself in Africa, or Turkestan, or Palestine, or any place with a name like candy, fruit, or
the Bible. Her father and her father's father had
been missionaries; they were ministers in Salem and

saw the sea as a natural road for what they believed. As Salem merchants traded spices and brass from and to Zanzibar, so they preached. Her brother and she had been born in Africa; she did not remember it, he did. She had been her father's daughter after he returned from the brighter parts of his life. When a little girl, she had grown among stories and artifacts from Africa and China, where her grandfather had been.

Michael began to run with the wind, which from where he floated high on the waves shot directly to shore, even though on the beach it was confused and blew his wife's skirts and apron in all directions in imitation of a real tempest. Despite the wind and waves this run would be easier than most because he did not have to tack. He could head straight for the inlet, building up speed, until he passed it with a breath of quick relief. He felt confident, as he had while traveling. When he traveled he was not knit to his possessions and made an implement to maneuver them. When in other parts of the world he felt light and comfortable, as a good man would doing something good and easy. He dreamed of traveling with Suzanna; he knew she wanted to see what he had seen, and when he had seen it he had wished for her to be by him. Without reasons it was really quite simple. He loved her and wanted to go places with her. His boat, beautifully made by his cousins who put double seams and double caulk to satisfy him, gained speed and seemed to nose itself to target. He felt always when running the inlet, or shooting the bar as the older men called it, that he knew himself, that

he and the boat had something in common, a solidar-
ity on the waves.

She finished opening the clams and went to stand
by the inlet, breathing more deeply as the wind
forced itself into her body. Michael was coming in.
She was frightened and happy. They were married
in the spring and they first made love in late April,
so that the month had been always in her eyes. That
night when the window was opened and she could
see the stars through it, they heard the small streams
and rivulets from the melting snow. Now her hands
were harder and she cursed easily, and often making
love had nothing whatsoever to do with the stars or
the brooks, but only the bed and the heat they raised,
so that even ten minutes after in the deep of quiet
they were not dry and they glistened. She wished
that she would not spend the rest of her life trying
to get the slight flamboyance one must have when
nineteen, that Michael had in the navy when he
spent time finding the round world, that she had not
had. He was older and had a time when he had
stretched and felt free, a time between the times of
a child and a man when he used his eyes so as to tire
his entire body, a time when he got drunk in Spain
and awoke in Sicily. As a woman she could never do
the same; the most she could do was to dream, and
she did, and sometimes (although she tried to shoo
the thought away and get it out of her mind) she
wished she were rid of him.

When Michael bought her a Kodak for Christmas,
she went around taking pictures of views, and buildings, and when photographing the town she had
wished that the streets had been clear of people. Her

album was filled at first with shots of seascapes, and
boats in a line, and ill-exposed sunsets, and angular
rocks by the ocean. But after a few months she
learned that people were necessary for photographs,
that their faces and their bodies made the best pictures. She tried to explain that to Michael but he understood only partially, because he was a man still
wed (and strongly so) to the landscape—it had been
his life. She felt this division between them the worst
fact of her life. He had been slow to her innovation.
She cursed at the wind and exhaled as if to express
her anger, as if to say "Damn him." She continued
dreaming of places where he had been and she had
not.

Michael was nearing the shore, his face set ever so
strongly in an expression that made her long for him
inexpressibly. It was like that of an Arab bedouin or
a Tartar charging over the plain on his horse, a soldier leading his battery or regiment in close-ordered
electrifying precision. His boat caught all the violence of the wind and went faster than it had ever
gone, breaking for the opening trimmed with heavy
deadening rocks.

She was full of love for him, and yet she had
thoughts of being a widow. Her fine imagination
presented to her a picture of a woman in black, so
beautifully blond and tanned, walking on the beach
or in a foreign city, a Mediterranean port, Strega, Os-
tuni, or Capri, shepherded by memories of her dead
husband whom she loved more than anything in the
world. She cried for him every night and turned
away gentle suitors by the score until the whole
world said in unison, "Look how fine she is, and how

good," and sucked in its cheeks and oceans in un-trammeled delight at her tight faith to her husband's ashes. She tried so hard not to think that way, but the thoughts came like waves into the bay, from some sort of sea where she had not been, and wished to go. She tensed with the love of the moment, for her husband was shooting the bar on a violent day in the bright autumn of her twentieth year.

He neared the bar and looked at the wind. His hands closed tightly on the ropes and tiller. Then a silence. She saw his face clearly. Everything was still and dark, with silence except for the gentle luffing of his white sails, and the freedom of her apron in the wind.

All her life and all that she had read flashed before her as she saw her husband's frail boat crash against the huge rocks. A part of her beauty vanished, and her dreaming was done.

Lightning North of Paris

It was approaching five o'clock on a cool afternoon in late October. Harry Spence sat on a stone railing in front of the Jeu de Paume, and as he waited for Shannon he looked through a maze of autumn trees stirred by a wind promising of winter and challenging in its direct cold northernness, a wind which lighted fires. Shannon was extremely tall and graceful. This, her face, and her dancer's body were a continual proclamation that she be taken dead seriously. In fact, anyone not always alert with her would find himself left behind as if in the slipstream of a fast train which had just passed. She stared other women down like a man; they often hated her. In a café she had the same effect as music or a fireplace, quickly becoming the center. Men were drawn to her because they did not immediately fall in love. Her power put them off until they got close enough and then went mad, leaving lovely wives and waiting for

Shannon on the street, where if she passed they became speechless as she crossed in leotards and a long skirt, a soft silk scarf trailing.

When Harry took up with Shannon he knew she would leave, but he was privileged to be with her for a time because he would not scare. He was always on guard, convincing her that he too was arbitrary and painfully free, as independent as a cloud sailing across frontiers. It was an act he put on successfully, but it was exhausting. Only a young man could have kept it up. He thought that if her demands had been made on a man older than twenty-five he would have died; frequency of intercourse was only a small part of the monumental task. That year was like a Channel swim. He wondered how he had done it, and how Shannon could always remain Shannon. They all moved like figures inside a furnace, which at the time was appropriate, and constructive, for they sat during the night at small desks and penned words or music, or played instruments, or painted, not knowing who was really good and who would fall back to the small towns of New York and Ohio never to be heard from again, perhaps to be unknown interpreters of those who had remained.

Harry Spence had not come to Paris because it was Paris, although once there he realized that even in imitation long after the originals (none of whom had really been first) the city was still a blaze and a dream. He had been granted a restricted fellowship stipulating that he live in a section of Paris dear to the benefactor and considered by him to be magical in its effect on musical composition. When flying into the city that September, he wished he were a writer of words rather than music. The prospect was stunning, spread white into the bordering fields. Masculine ministries enclosed luxurious gardens of mathematical green—from the air this appeared to be the hallmark of the city. He had had the feeling that he was returning to the vortex of civilization, having indeed been there before, that the inhabitants were possessed of a strange combination of clarity and feeling and were at that moment lighting fires over secret magnetic zones which crisscrossed the earth, making artists, and converged at Paris in the center of wheat and wine-filled French prairies sobered and chilled by blasts from the North.

Wherever children gather at a forge or fire, its red heat giving them warmth in darkness, they learn quickly principles of art. This is what Harry had thought when very young as he sat by a fire with his father and uncle and grandfather in the middle of violet autumn fields which they knew would see frost by morning. The grandfather had passed through Paris on his way to the front; the father and uncle had crossed the Seine riding on the same tank. They had ached from their hearts to see Paris in peace, to live and work there. They had carried cartridges through Saint-Germain-des-Prés and been continually on edge and nervous, for they then were sent to bosky woods near the German border to fight and kill. After his father returned, his life had calmed. He never yearned for the war, but he knew it had made him. There was plenty of thunder in the following peace, haystack-leveling winds to test him, obstacles to his dreams, but none of this later adversity had defined and shaped him as had the war. He wished with all his might that he would not communicate this to his son, that the boy, born after the fighting, would find other means to know himself and would not repeat the horror for the sake of becoming a man. He wished for his son peaceful storms and not the waxen white light of artillery duels. He prayed for this. And Harry *was* different, soft, a baby beyond his time, unknowing of combat and the continual deathly backdrop of war, an almost effeminate university-bred tortoise-shell-glassed composer of music. His father and uncle, the survivors of that session by the fire, rejoiced that he would be thrust into the heart of Paris in a piping time of peace, peace, said the uncle a veteran of four years of solid war, peace, God bless it.

He set up in a small apartment overlooking the Champ de Mars and on the first day of autumn when the returning population was in full frenzy, in a copper-colored bar where he stopped early in the morning to drink chocolate and eat pieces of buttered bread which he paid for as he took them one by one off a round plate, as the streets were washed down and men in blue coats streamed in and out, he looked across the room to a bank of sunny windows where the white dusty light was coming in on Shannon and made her look like an Irishwoman in a Sargent portrait.

Because she was so beautiful in her enlightened posture and expression, and because an intelligence radiated from her, he became very daring and approached the table, cup of chocolate in hand, a beautiful leather briefcase under one arm. He said, *"Sprechen Sie Deutsch?"* at which she smiled and

then laughed, because if they had been two Texas
longhorns standing there in the corner of the café it
could not have been more obvious that both were
Americans; the fact was like water pouring over a
dam. They went out and walked away hours. His daring began to extend itself for a year's tenure. He fell
in love with her, having the peculiar feeling which
new kisses can bring, an overwhelming sense of
being alive in the face of the present. The world became an energetic frame. It was almost like being the
leading man in an opera. Within a week she had
moved two wicker trunks into his apartment. She did
ballet exercises in the middle of the floor while they
talked. She could not have told him that the first
night when they walked up the Champs-Élysées and
basked in the lights and September fountains, a
red-bearded Rumanian architect sat staring at her
former bed and cursed himself in Hungarian,
French, and English, and eventually threw a glass
full of Scotch flat up against the wall.

And then she disappeared each morning and came
back only after dark, having danced every day down
to exhaustion. Harry was writing music, at which he
was becoming masterful, in which he was beginning
to be able to do anything he wanted. By terrifying
bouts of sustained work he was forcing the creation
of a great bed of experience, so that in the strong
frame and healthy body of his twenties could be
found an old man who had lived since the turn of the
century, and whose wisdom at the craft astounded
and amazed even competitors and the nearly deaf.
He could write pieces as deep and blue as a fjord,
echoing and quiet, and he could write as red as he

pleased, American jazz born of a rich heartland and
the death of the wilderness. And strangely, the better he got, the better he got, with no chance of slip-
ping. This stood even Shannon in awe. Once he had
said, I can do anything, absolutely anything. I am almost a master, and she had looked mean and tough
and said, You can do *nothing*, leaving the room in
a fit of envy which meant he could have her for at
least another six months until their powers evened
out again and she was able to glide and swirl naturally and gracefully beyond the ecstatic points to
which his labor had taken him. But he was going farther, and they both knew it.

Winter passed. They had an enormous electricity
bill, for the lights burned late at night, with Harry
bearing down on his blinding white music pads and
then touching the piano as if he were stroking a
horse. Shannon danced and danced, slept from exhaustion, and danced again, becoming like Harry one
of the ones who did not return in quiet and sadness
to the starting point with a series of exquisite memories and some first editions. She danced at the Na-
tional Theater. His pieces were really performed.
Sometimes he conducted, in a light gray and blue
tweed suit and his tortoise-shell glasses, and when he
turned at the close and faced an approving audience,
their feet stamping, the timbers of the hall shaking
as if the earth had quaked, it threw him off balance
for weeks during which he stuffed himself with good
food and could write only music which was so
squeaky it sounded like rusty wheels in the high Gare
du Nord, music which if played for the pigeons would

have made them rise in intolerance and bend in a
sheet of white and gray across the plane of Paris sky.

And he ran in the afternoon amid the blue which
met buildings softly under the clouds, panting, pushing his glasses back on his face as they tried to fall
to the ground. Eventually he built a routine of going
all the way out to Neuilly and back, and as he got
stronger it wrote Shannon in for another few months,
for she could love only strength and could not face
weakness. But it was so hard, to run and write, to eat
like a beast and then starve, to make love until the
dawn and then be fit only for the morgue, to be
moved so by the music that it was like an electrocu-
tion, complete surrender and exhaustion.

That summer they went to Greece. The winter's
rain seemed as far away as medieval European cities,
and yet it was in one of these cities that Harry wrote
in thundering clear classical style. He took the opportunity to take down good Greek music, and to write
barrelhouse rolls to limericks they made up. These
became extremely popular at a restaurant in Nea
Epidavros called "Yellow House of Nonsensical Pleasure" where the foreigners gathered in the evenings.
Of several dozen Swedes, Englishmen, French,
Greeks, Americans, and Italians, three had birthdays
on the same day, two (including Harry) had perfect
pitch, all knew the fountain at Aix-en-Provence (or
said they did), and everyone except the women except one was in love with Shannon—as if drawn into
the maelstrom; the bright challenge took them up in
its hands like moths.

Harry and Shannon slept on the roof; a phono-
graph played them to sleep. As they watched the

stars they became separate. Harry knew she was in love with the doctor, an Oklahoman who had been broken in Vietnam and then come back stronger. He was both larger and wiser than Harry, although he could not compose music, and he called Harry "Spence." Next to him Harry felt like a young midget, and because he was not fresh or new at Shannon's game he lost early on in the subtle war of deferences at the Yellow House of Nonsensical Pleasure. Harry retired to the piano and played his barrelhouse rolls, and then stopped going there altogether, and then Shannon did not come up to the roof.

He cursed himself for not having the wisdom war brings. His father had told him of lying awake in an open meadow with an automatic rifle across his lap, waiting for the enemy while the sky was filled with artillery flashes and the white lightning of battle, a terror which numbed the little patrol in the field, something Harry might never know. It was one of the major reasons Harry loved his father, his sense early on that the man knew terror and bloodshed, and was grateful and loving just to be alive. They, the men in his family who had started out as merchants and professors and been made into warriors, knew something he could not. But they envied him for his cradle of peace. There was no way to compete with the Oklahoman, with the bronzed face and tranquil eyes which had seen men die in war. Harry was at a loss but determined to push with the same energy which had led them to survive, toward a depth in peace *they* could never know. He too was a fighter of sorts. To take in the whole great compass of the world—this was his task. The expanse of it could kill, and he had to dodge as best he could the potent back-lash of music's ecstasy. He left for Paris precipitously, almost without thinking or looking back, and when he arrived he forwarded Shannon her wicker trunks, wondering what she would do with twenty-five pairs of dancing shoes in a wild rocky spine of the Peloponnesus. She had written that if she returned she would meet him at the Jeu de Paume at five o'clock on October 27, the day after her ticket expired.

It was already five-thirty. He could smell roasting chestnuts. He was in his light gray and blue suit, and he carried the leather briefcase under his arm. It was filled with musical manuscripts he had written since his return from Greece. He was steady, slept soundly, spoke softly, and smiled more. He was older, and felt like his father, enjoying little things. His desk looked more chestnut-colored, and the bright lights of autumn were sharper than they had ever been. He knew now who was good, and he knew he was good. Massive clouds made the dark come early. Cold lightnings could be seen far north of Paris. High in the air birds rode thermals, tiny white flecks against the gray clouds. He loved the cool air, and looked up and down the paths, but they were emptying and the leaves just rustled on the floor of the Tuileries as if they were a German forest. That night he would sit under his lamp and pen the blinding white sheets; every day he felt himself rising a little higher, quietly, powerfully. He jumped off the railing and walked toward the Champs-Élysées. He was due at dinner with a friend whose sister was to be there. He was in the Ministry of Finance and she was a model who had appeared on the covers of *Match, Jours de*

France, and *Elle.* One evening Harry had been in a restaurant alone and had stared at her picture, feeling himself fall into a trance somehow allied to the sweet darkness outside. My God, he said, as his heart opened to her image. The serenity was numbing. He found himself walking with quick step as a winter wind came down the Champs-Élysées.

He passed a tall girl with a beret. That bittersweet frame and the cold rushing air, the leaves like percussion, made him shudder. His friend's sister had deep blue eyes and on the cover of *Elle* she had been wearing a blue velvet gown. He knew he would be loving her soon, in the quiet of autumn, smooth, silent, and blue.

Mountain Dancing in Truchas

A fashion in New Mexico was mountain dancing, which was called that because it started in small villages in the North up high in the mountains. Rarely were there clouds in Truchas. Farther on toward Truchas Peak were thick forests with clear steady streams. Perpetually terrified of bears, cattle roamed the mountains, meek beasts who looked with fear even at one another and at birds, and who at the slightest noise would crash through the thick brush and run until they dropped—because like young children in the dark they feared their own sounds.

Mountain dancing was not a *form* of dancing but rather just dancing on a Friday night. Couples would come, and if not couples then people alone. And they often brought their children. Josie brought her children because they were little enough to fear the moon and the night silence over the desolate black and white hillsides. They played in the corner with several other little children, some of whom were in bathrobes. All moved much faster because of the music, although they did not themselves know it.

Josie was tall and brown. Around her wrists were bracelets of dull silver studded with blue stones. This work of the Southwest was nothing when compared to her eyes; her eyes, black and Persian against the red clay and outstanding clear green of the trees. When she held her hand, fingers spread, over her breast so that the tips of her nails reached nearly to her neck, it was possible to see her eyes reflected in her bracelets, and the silver and turquoise were also to be seen in the wet blue-black of her eyes, although not as well.

She danced the best of all the women in Truchas, and better than the unattached girls. Dancing was a matter of pride and slow movements, of watching a wall or window while in the mind there was soaring and flying over silver mountain ranges, standing up rigid with the wind and rain rushing by as if around an upright Christ. The more ecstasy, the more still-ness. That is why they started with much movement and the pine floor rocked, resinous, yellow, and dusty. At evening's end very little was left of motion, for everything was contained, and the wind whistling over the roof made the women shudder with love. But Josie was alone, for her husband had died in the army. She had considered other men even before the time of mourning had passed, because she had loved him so much, and chose to start when she wished since she would never allow herself to be a horse breaking at the bit, and her legitimate pride made her seek others as an exercise in grief.

He had been in the First Cavalry. He was Spanish, from Truchas for many generations, mixed with the dying Indians. He had the same dark eyes, and he had killed many men before he himself was killed in a helicopter crash.

She did love him, more so when he was dead, and she had loved him in that cold way which is the great love of one who is hurt. But then, there were wonderful clear moments, all lightness and gaiety, such as one time when they walked for miles down the road in the moonlight just laughing and relieved that they had nowhere to go and were completely alone.

When he died she learned much and she became more protective of her children. She became then not a girl but a woman. There are ways in which a woman becomes a woman; they often take her by great surprise, and this was one. It seemed to her that she valued her own life a little less, and life itself much more. She became devoted to her children and would have made sacrifices for them of which a year or even a few months before she would not have dreamed. She felt old, but very strong, and when old people went by in the street she understood them more, and was proud of them.

One Friday night in the summer there was mountain dancing. Josie was there. She and her children had been escorted by the man who guided hunters from the East, and spent much time alone in the mountains. People were somewhat afraid of him because he was so strong and was seldom in the village, but at the same time they were happy to have him because they guessed that he would fight hard for them if for any reason they had to fight. Josie was enlivened by his company because he was so much older. It seemed to her girlfriends, whom she had already outdistanced, that he was frightening and somehow beyond understanding. It was an important time for her. She was learning to change her sadness into a tenderness which made itself manifest on nights just like these. The pain had withered to a point of beauty, and she was receptive and full of love.

When things began to go and she stared no longer at the black glass through which were tinted stars and shapes of peaks, when in fact she was eating a lemon ice and talking convivially with her friends and a young boy who had come up from Santa Fe to work for the summer on his cousin's farm, two men came in, two strangers. They smiled occasionally but seemed not to have come for the dance.

Josie began dancing with the hunter, who was a good dancer. A time passed while she danced and was very happy. Then, when the musicians rested, the two men went to the middle of the floor and asked for attention. In Truchas no one had to *ask* for attention. If he wanted to speak to the people all at once, he spoke. These young men were from California, their Spanish was not the same, and they said they were revolutionaries. One spoke, and then the other said that what he said was true. They talked of fighting, and guns, and violence. And they mentioned many times "the people." They talked for half an hour, and when they finished there was silence in the room. The hunter was unimpressed, and smiled at them as if they were children who knew very little. What did they know of the mountains, of

the peaks? They were from the flat land and not ac-
customed to the thin air. The other people were puz-
zled, and did not understand fully what they had said
or why.

But Josie tightened her lips and tensed herself to
stop the shaking. She was furious, and looked at the
children in the corner and gathered her own with
her eyes. With her head held high and the tendons
in her long slim arms raised, she stepped out a pace
and challenged the two young men. She threw back
her black hair.

What did they know, she said, about Truchas,
about mountain country. A few years ago a man from
the army had come and convinced her husband to
fight, making him believe that he would be fighting
for himself and for his children. "These are his children," she said, sweeping her arm toward the now
still babies stacked in the arms of older women who
had taken them up. "They are there and quite alive
and do not need to be fought for. Their father is dead
because of men like you. You are not revolutionaries.
There is nothing new about you. You are the leaders
of men and the slaughterers of men. I myself have
seen you pass through this village before, and I will
not be fooled a second time."

The hunter stepped forward, but Josie waved him
back. With the eyes of a lioness she looked at the two
men and she was full of rage. On this the night when
she began to learn how to make life whole again, they
had come to tear it apart. She would not let these
men take her children as they had taken her husband. She would fight all right, she would fight for
herself, she said, because *she was the people*. "And

it is time," she said, "that all the people learn to fight just for themselves, and not for anyone but themselves. Truchas remains here, and you will leave. Pass on. Leave us." The young men began to argue, saying first that they understood her feelings . . .

"You do *not* understand," she said. The Mayor, a little old man with a pink face and only one good eye, said politely that Friday night was for mountain dancing, and that if the two young men wished they could come to the same place on any first day of the month and air their views at the town meeting. He asked them very cordially if they would like to dance, at which the previously silent hall exploded with laughter, and all the people of Truchas laughed for a long time. And then they ate, and when the musicians started to play they danced, and that night many would make love and some only dream of it, and on the morrow herd cattle and chop wood, and the hunter would again disappear into the mountains.

Josie danced with tears in her eyes. Her bracelets jangled and she was happy and full of love. The two young men started the long walk down to Santa Fe.

Leaving the Church

"I have never been as calm in my life," said Father Trelew. "No, not ever." He was speaking to Helen, his housekeeper, but she was not much in his mind, even though she had been with him for several years—he could not remember exactly how many. He looked at the sky. "Soon I will be on the plane to New York, and then to Rome."

"Have you been to Rome before, Father?"

"Yes, I have, in 1925 when Mussolini was in power. You know what I think of him, don't you, don't you, Helen."

"I most certainly do."

It was hot where they stood, but his clothes were clean and white and his thick hair was white, so he had no discomfort. There was a black spot of oil on the drive. A shimmering desert stretched beyond—his parish. He could smell the hot sand and see waves of heat rising from it, distorting the mountains.

The driver put the bags in the car, and after bidding goodbye to Helen and shaking her hand Father Trelew got in the back and clicked the door shut. The car was air-conditioned. It was taking him to Phoenix for the plane. He was going to Vatican II.

It was years since he had left his parish. In New York before his parents died, they had called him sometimes "The Indian Priest," but he never heard them, they thought. They were ashamed of him. They wanted him to be an archbishop. Instead he spoke to deep-brown faces in a dark church with no lighting, while the sand blew outside. He could see it through the window sometimes—perfectly white against the blue sky and billowing like foam on the ocean, and yet it was cool and dry. His mother and father thought he would come back from Arizona as if from some foreign campaign, distinguished and likely to advance. The bishops would appreciate his sacrifice. He knew he was not coming back, but he never told his parents. They died in the Depression, sure that at the end of the Depression he would be called back from Arizona.

If he thought about being an archbishop, he clenched his fist and banged it on the table. When he had too much to drink, he thought wild thoughts about seeing God, about golden staircases and whitened plumes rising from the wide floor of Heaven, about places where it was so bright you couldn't see anything at all. He had such prideful dreams only after wine or whiskey, so he drank rarely.

He arrived in Rome early in the morning. He felt

young, for he had slept on the plane and Rome
seemed to him not to have changed since 1925, when
he was thirty and had been there for two months as
a student. Now there were few carriages, but the
streets were the same. In Piazza Navona, the old colors still stood; the fountains had been going for almost forty years since he first saw them. He wondered if they ever stopped, for even a moment.
Perhaps each time the city died—after the March,
or when the Germans were there—the fountains
stopped. He thought to ask an old man, but realized
that no one man would have watched constantly, and
besides, he thought, I am an old man and could tell
no one if ever in Arizona the mountains turned pure
white or the sky the color of gold, because I have not
watched them the whole time. At least, the fountains
appear never to stop; at least, I have seen them while
they were going.

His budget for this trip was delightfully large. The
Vatican paid much of it, his diocese another great
part, and his savings the rest. He thought he would
live for this short time in a fashion unlike that of his
small frame house on the reservation. There the
wind came in a steady stream through an unputtied
crack of the window. In the morning gold light
glinted off his porcelain shaving basin. At these times
there was only silence and cold. After he shaved, he
opened the window, and after he opened the window he dressed and prayed—but not in Rome. He
would pray, yes, but in Rome he would pray in his
own good time. There would be no kneeling on hard
wooden floors, no fasting, and no cold.

He checked in at the Grand Hotel, which was full

of priests and extremely elegant—marble, rich Oriental rugs, chandeliers, and in his room French doors with a view of a piazza and its enormous fountain shooting a hundred feet upward. As the weeks passed, he habitually ate his breakfast on the balcony. With high winds, he felt slight droplets of spray from the fountain. His bed was large, with a satin quilt. As always when he stayed in hotels—even in Phoenix—he wondered what people had made love in the bed, and then laughed good-naturedly at himself. He had learned to live with *that* a long time ago.

Father Trelew's role at the Council was not very exciting; indeed, the Council itself was not very exciting. He was just a priest. From where he sat near the entrance of St. Peter's the Pope was only a white spot and the Dove of the Holy Ghost a needlepoint of light—a ray. When he removed his glasses, the sea of cardinals before the Pope was a mass of red, and when they stood their motion made them look like red waves. They were seated on both sides of the aisle. It was as if Moses had spread them back into the galleries. But whom would Father Trelew tell? Helen? Helen thought only of her child, who broke windows and stayed alone in the hills at night even when it was cold. Perhaps Father Wohlen from Los Angeles, who was Father Trelew's friend simply because they were both at the Grand Hotel; Father Wohlen had an idea that anyone from west of the Mississippi was somehow a loving brother. But Father Trelew did not like Father Wohlen, for he ate too much and had an unconvincing laugh. There was no one to tell. "There is no one to tell," he said. "Maybe

I will sketch it." He had not sketched since he had last been in Rome. He was in a drawing class then. He was mainly interested in architectural form; Rome offered him that, while the desert did not. He had tried to paint the Indians and the things they did, but there was not much left of them by that time, and he suspected not much left of him—or, rather, of his talent to draw.

Did he dare begin again? "I must," he said, the blood coursing to his face. The hair at his temples was silver. When his face lit up, he looked like giltwork. I am the only priest in the world, he thought, who looks like a church. He would have to buy a pad and charcoal.

One day, he left the Council early and began to walk back to his hotel. He passed through Piazza Navona, and somewhere off it on a side street he found an art store. "Could I have," he began but found that he was not able to speak the words. "Could I have . . ." and then, like a madman, he rushed from the shop.

He was disturbed by this, knowing precisely what it was. He tried not to think, flooding his mind with words that formed in silence on his lips, like the cries of men in dreams of sinking ships. "Flood it with good cheer. Fill it up, fill it up, for life is short." If he could somehow get supplies, he could sit by the fountain and sketch.

What is the power of a priest's life? It is that he need not fear. "Father Wohlen," he said next day, too nervously, "do you think that on the way back from the Cathedral tomorrow you could stop in an art shop and get me a large pad and some charcoal?" He gasped for breath. "Because I must stay late for chapel vespers. I don't mean to trouble you . . ."

"No trouble, no trouble," said Father Wohlen. "I'll do it. You just give me the money, tell me where to go, and I'll do it."

Father Trelew did not go to vespers; he did not even go to the Council that day. It was an important day, too. He stayed in his room, and it seemed to him that God was working wonders with his body. If he had been a proud man, he might have presumed that he was undergoing Divine revelation, that he was receiving saintly visions. Only once in his life, only once, had the test of his body responded to his mind and made him tremble. No, it was the body responding to the *heart* which caused trembling.

He sat on the edge of his bed, with his glasses off, and the blur of outside sunlight made him feel the enlivened world. "Oh my God, my dear God," he prayed, "I am not having visions, am I?" He said this to a shaft of sunlight in his room at his feet, and the golden dust danced in center beam.

When Father Wohlen gave him his materials, Father Wohlen thought Trelew was sick. Something was wrong with the man.

Father Trelew ran his hands over the pad, took the charcoal out of its box, and felt the smooth rectangular blocks. The cool of the blocks reminded him of the desert at evening, their blackness of the night, but the night was full of white stars. That was an advantage he would not have had as an archbishop—seeing the Milky Way stretched as a shimmering band over the great dome of his little life. The power of a priest's life is that he is unafraid. All is concele-

bration. "I am beginning to realize this," said Father
Trelew. "That all is concelebration—all of the city,
all of the stars. The Church is for me. A man need
not fear his loneliness. He need not fear his loneliness, for God is strong and all is concelebration. The
power of a priest's life is that he need not fear."

The next day he was up very early. He read most
of *La Stampa*. A bus took him to the Vatican.

It would not be right for him to sketch in the Cathedral. His idea was to study a particular scene and
commit it to memory for drawing. Back in Arizona,
he would paint it. Somehow he got very close to the
Pope. Though it was thrilling to see him, it was not
the Pope he chose to study but the undersecretaries
close to the Papal Throne, seated at a table next to
the balustrade of the Confessio.

Another priest from America was determined to
guide him. "That is Bishop Wilhelm Kempf of Lim-
burg," he said, "and Archbishop Villot of Lyons,
Archbishop Krol of Philadelphia, and the archbishop
of Madrid—I do not know his name."

"Thank you, thank you," said Father Trelew to the
other priest, who wanted to say more, and then to
escape he stepped much closer to the scene than he
would ordinarily have dared. He was the foremost
of observers; between him and the undersecretaries
was only a slight and terrible plain of marble. The
Pope was not far. I am so near greatness, he thought.
Princes! He studied the scene. He had always had a
good architectural memory. He was fine on detail,
but here he was impressed by grandeur, which was
glowing, descript, calling out to any man.

Entrenched in the blackness of distant high walls,

the red table of the undersecretaries glowed scarlet; ringed with gold and tasseled, its colors moved in front of the eyes. The undersecretaries, in pure white with upswinging conical hats of flattened design, did not rest upon their red ribbons banded about them in curves and sweeps like water falling. They worked at papers, and they were in different positions, so that the tall conical hats pointed together in a smooth indication, like the crest of a wave, to the Pope. And beyond them was a swirling black column edged with a rotating blade of gold. It was so bright it made Father Trelew shudder. He stood for a good half hour, intent upon the secretaries. His gaze was powerful. He was having the time of his life, for he knew he would soon begin to draw.

One of the Papal secretaries noticed Father Trelew when he first came, and then again after half an hour. He thought perhaps he was wanted and crossed the forbidden marble at a glide. His robes were such that his feet did not seem to move. "Is there anything I can do for you, Father?" he said curiously.

Father Trelew, who had tried and failed to escape when he saw the bishop coming, could not answer. His steadfastness had provoked the great man, but he could not answer. His mouth hung open.

"Are you all right?" the bishop asked. He laughed pleasantly and touched Father Trelew, who felt again like sinking ships, and whose mouth was still open while the bishop returned to his table, silent and smiling.

Father Trelew managed to close his mouth as he walked back into the crowd. Everyone looked at him as if he were in some way connected to the Pope. He might have enjoyed that had he been able to answer the bishop, but he was expressionless and numb. And yet he did not panic. He wanted to get back to the hotel to draw, and then the next day to Piazza Navona, with his pad, to sketch the central fountain. He could use his material freely there. He was marvelously excited. He quickly forgot the incident with the bishop, bent down to tie his shoe, and strode like a master through St. Peter's to home in the hotel. He did not think, Oh, I am such a little man, until he arrived in his room and could not draw what he had remembered.

Father Trelew had many times told weeping Indian women that sleep helped the troubled. He had many times watched tears travel down a face like wind-cut brown granite—sparkling black eyes in the church's dimness—and thought how deeply the woman would sleep. Always the next day he saw her going about her business, which is precisely what *he* did the next day.

Late in the afternoon, he found himself in Piazza Navona. He thought to draw the fountain and the buildings vanishing in perspective, to test his draftsmanship. He planned to have dinner at one of the restaurants there so popular with Roman families (fairly well-to-do, he assumed) and clerics, and perhaps find an acquaintance with whom to chat as it got dark.

He took a seat at one of the smaller fountains and put his legs up on the stone wall. In his freshly pressed white suit he looked as if he might have been a missionary from the Congo or Asia. "Perhaps they think I am a jungle priest," he said happily. "But I am not a jungle priest, I am a desert priest—and how many of those are there? Very few in the Sahara, none, as far as I know, in the Gobi, and none in the Nafud. That leaves me, and a few others. I should find out who they are, write to them, perhaps start a journal."

He was a good priest, and did his job well. He thought of photographers he had seen on the reservation, who paid people small sums to be photographed and recorded their humiliation and discomfort only to pass it off to the world as the pathos of humankind. In the operations of caring for his flock, Father Trelew tried to avoid the photographers' fallacy. Only rarely did tragedy face them. There were complaints and sorrows, but not much passionate loss. He had to accept that. It was a small population, and not a battlefield—he was *truly* needed once in a great while, but he refused to buy the illusion that when they came to him aching from life in the world he was doing great service. In that way, when he did great service he felt he could vault over mountains. In other words, he was a lean man.

He thought, My dreams can be dreamed in forty-five minutes, and then I become either tired or empty and stop dreaming—again, leanness. In the weakening sun he began to sketch Piazza Navona, and his hand moved rapidly, surprising him with what it had remembered. He included cars and carriages, and the horses, drawn well. After several hours, when it was dark, he closed his pad and put a little piece of charcoal into the box, which he then put in his pocket. Putting the box in his pocket was like the sheriff putting his gun back in his holster after a shoot-out. When he swung his legs back to the ground it was as if they had boots and spurs. He had drawn the Piazza, and it was therefore his.

With dinner, he ordered a bottle of white wine. He was not used to it; it was a mistake, he told himself halfway through, but drank it anyway. Then everything began to fall into place as he watched the lights of Rome in the heat of September and wandered about like a young drunk.

He was a good-natured man, had always been a good-natured man. His father, who was ambitious for him to the point of hating him, said once, "Michael, what have you got, what the hell have you got?" Father Trelew had wanted to reply that he was a good man, could draw, and loved God. But he wept instead, and only later, half weeping, did he say to his mother, "Tell him, by my honor, that I am just a man," and left for the train to the West.

He was good-looking. He had a wonderful face. Even at his age, and he was almost seventy, women were not unmoved by his glance. When he was younger they had frequently fallen in love with him, especially the troubled ones, who always fall for priests of one sort or another. There had been one in Rome in 1925, when he was thirty and had rebuffed already a good many trouble-seekers and those testing their power. A priest is familiar with that. He can handle that. It is the guileless ones, the ones who really love, who make things difficult.

In 1925, the library of the old Accademia was framed
with sea-green reader's lamps, which glowed in the
day. The walls were so old one might have been sorry
for them had they not been painted with angels, gardens, and bursting suns.

Father Trelew was not merely appreciative but ecstatic. He often stayed in the library all day and well
into the evening. He was writing a paper on Oderisi
da Gubbio, a miniaturist of the thirteenth century.
When he left the library he saw only the colors he
had seen all day in illuminated manuscripts. It
seemed to him that he sailed home without a word,
simply gliding and brimming.

One was assigned a seat, and results were not always pleasing. Harvard undergraduates dying for the
sunburnt girl in purple who sometimes wore black
were placed across the room from her facing the
other way into a bunch of nuns. Father Trelew could
hardly breathe for two weeks; he was the only man
at a table for Radcliffe girls. One of them fell in love
with him, just by looking.

"What is your name . . . Father?" she asked, since
there was no one else at the table.

"Michael Trelew," he said, frightenedly.

"And where are you from?"

"From. From. I'm from Ossining, New York. Perhaps you have heard of us—I mean it, as it is the
home of Sing Sing Prison. Where are you from?"

"Forty-nine East Eighty-sixth Street," she said,
waiting.

His fear was beginning to bore him, and in anger
he wanted to be reckless, if only not to be dull. But
he could only stare at her. She was thin, and blond.

He could not decide if she looked like the Madonna. She was very brown and her dress was white.

She said, and with her green eyes. "Can we eat together tonight?" It was for her a difficult request, and she blushed. She felt like what she thought of popular music—brash but finally very beautiful. She was embarrassed by her own directness, expectant, and altogether very open and tender.

Father Trelew was taken. Yet he answered as if from a prepared hollowness, "I have no money. I am a priest . . ." He hesitated, because he was no longer interested in what he was saying. Instead, visions of neutral Switzerland flashed at him and he entertained the profoundly impossible notion of running away with this girl.

The weeks that followed were very sad for both of them. They were both gaining, but they were also losing, and perhaps what united them so strongly at first was that they felt they knew what the other was relinquishing. And then they had that particular camaraderie which exists among schoolboys, soldiers, and outlaws.

It did not take long before they were speeding to Switzerland in a touring car he had rented with the remainder of his grant for study in Rome. He told her the speedometer's thin red needle reminded him of a hummingbird's tongue. They stopped at a dam in a valley of the Alps. Across the spillway was an automobile bridge that led nowhere, and fog from the rushing water cascaded in a convection arch over the bridge, over the two of them.

The time together in Rome had made the priest and the girl heady. She was young, and he not so young but it was new to him. When he removed his collar he sighed in relief and walked out into the warm sun where she was waiting in the open car in a hat and heavy coat ready to head north. There was singing all the way. In one inn, Father Trelew, having had too much wine, told the porter that he was a priest. The porter raised his arms as if to say, "That is very serious, but so what?"

They stayed in Switzerland for more than a month. He was going to give up the Church, when she left him. There was no comfort. Everything had failed. He had not written his paper and could show nothing for his summer in Italy. The bishops at home would have his head for that. There would be nothing he could say; he could see himself gaping at them.

It would not be the first time he had found himself mute. The first was the time he and the girl had been unable to resolve an argument and it grew wider and wider, until she was on a platform waiting for a train and nothing he could say made anything better. He felt untrained for that sort of thing. The argument had started while they were drawing by a lake, and he threw his picture to the ground. He was angry. She had too many plans for him. She had him in the White House when he was not yet even just a defrocked priest. He threw his picture on the ground because he realized that she was young and nothing could be done about it. When the train came, she was crying, for she did love him, and perhaps because she was crying and she was young she struck a blow she had not meant to strike. She was not even Catholic but Episcopalian. She said through the steam and rain which soaked them both and was warm and very much like their tears—she said on that hot misty August day so uncommon for Switzerland, "And you are such a little man." It was then that his mouth dropped open and he could say nothing. She cried and cried, and as the train left he ran after it half-heartedly with his mouth still open and tears streaming down his cheeks and the steam from the gaskets making his suit smell as if it had been just pressed.

He looked at the high white mountains, and his smallness choked him. He boarded the next train to Rome after waiting in the station for seventeen hours. He did not eat, nor did he return for his belongings. It stayed misty and warm until he left.

They sent him to Arizona. They would have thrown him out, but they needed someone there. He was perfect for the job. He could have left on his own. They offered him that, but he was afraid. The archbishop made him afraid. Offices made him afraid. Even cathedrals now made him afraid.

The only thing that calmed him was the desert and its silent, dry heat. In the desert he started to seek God as he had not ever sought Him. In some ways he stayed weak, and in others he became very strong.

He watched the blue mountains and the billowing sand, which was like the foam on the ocean when he came home from Italy, but cool and dry.

A man from the desert is not a dry man, but he keeps what is wet inside him, like a cactus, so that visitors to him wonder how in such a world he can be alive and have enough. Father Trelew had not been born in the desert, but his forty years there taught him much. Although there will be some who might deny that a man may be taught such a thing, it is a fact that Father Trelew was calm, quiet, and gracious during his first heart attack. It occurred while he dined with several other American priests near the hotel in a restaurant they had all frequented during the first weeks of the Council, and then abandoned, then remembered and rushed to, as Father Trelew had done with his drawing. He ate prosciutto and melon, *scaloppine alla zingara,* and drank gaseous mineral water and cold white wine. He was contemplating dessert and had his wineglass raised to his lips when he felt the first pain. It seemed as if the entire restaurant had been jolted by an earthquake, and the electricity somehow savagely unleashed to attack the assembled priests. At first he thought there *had* been an earthquake. He kept his glass to his lips, afraid to move. He would put it down, slowly. He would go without dessert, excuse himself, and walk to see a doctor. He did not want to trouble his companions, because they were younger and he felt they did not like him; he had said hardly a thing in the course of the meal while they burned with the politics of Council.

But he could not move his arm to put his glass down. It was there for a full minute and no one noticed until he fell to the ground, for he could not stand the second wave. He fell to the ground still with the glass in his hand, apologizing and begging the pardon of the assembled priests, who were younger and who had ignored him.

When he awakened in his hospital room, he was grateful that the walls were not white. Rome is a yellow color, an old saffron-powdered sun color which seems always rising upward. His room was a comforting beige, the color of a lightly done roll in the oven.

He was happy to be alive and would not move his head until later, when a nun told him it was safe. He saw by turning his eyes the tops of pine trees and green hills in the not so far distance. He judged himself to be on a mountaintop. "Splendid," he said. "I'm on a mountaintop." He could hear birds and the clicking of crutches in the garden. After a few weeks he was up and about. He could see most of Rome from the garden and some of Rome came up to meet him, although that part of Rome which traveled up the hillside to him was not people but houses and streets.

When he had been a priest in Arizona and visited parishioners in the hospital, he thought because of its bustle and crowded corridors that a hospital was a social place. He had often thought of going to a hospital on some physical excuse to cure his loneliness, but in Rome (and he assumed that hospitals were spiritually the same everywhere) he discovered himself more alone than he had ever been. The face of his nurse was constantly changing, and there were eight doctors who cared for him in varying degree, none with particular intensity. He was alone during the day, and in the night. He did not dare draw. He was afraid to look in the mirror. No one paid him any attention, because he was old.

There was a man dying of some unknown disease, a violinist in a symphony orchestra in the north of Italy. He looked as if he were made of old loops and patches. He smelled of death. It came from inside him—from his bowels, from his throat, even from his legs and fingers. Father Trelew had smelled the same smell in Arizona when some boys cut open a deer they had shot in the mountains several days before. Every day the violinist sat in the garden and played. He was particularly fond of the Andante of Prokofiev's Second Violin Concerto, and he played it again and again. The officials allowed it because it helped those who recovered recover, those who were dying to die, and those in the middle of the road to pass the time. Father Trelew wanted to talk to the man whose music was so beautiful; he had never before heard any Prokofiev. When he went to him in the garden, he found the old man unable to speak. But the patterns of the music were so strongly ingrained, and his hands so powerful, that he played, he played, until the day of his death—not always correctly, often out of time, but always with much passion.

Father Trelew was not afraid of dying. He was afraid of what he might be before he died. When he first realized that he was dying he stayed in his chair—an old man in a chair—and tried frantically to remember all the parts of his life. He thought that when a man dies a man reviews what he has seen. He expected memories to jolt his frame, and visions to seek him and turn him, and shower the room with light.

But it just didn't happen as he expected, which he might have expected but did not. He became whimsical, prided himself suddenly on his sense of humor, and found the truth in sayings. He would say, "Love makes the world go round," and laugh. He was generally good-natured. Every four hours a nurse, never the same one, came to ask him if he had moved his bowels. He thought this was hilarious.

"Father Trelew."

"Yes, Sister."

"Have you moved your bowels in the last four hours?"

"Moved them where?" he said, and burst out laughing.

He was happy for no particular reason, and for that reason he adjudged himself particularly happy. One would have thought he was getting better. He said, "I want to have a good time on earth while I can," and spent the days in the garden, in the sun, watching flowers and delighting in the smell of rich grass, which was green as if on a riverbank. At night, he looked from his window at Rome, and because he remembered his memories so well he did not think of them, or need to. One look at Rome from a moderate distance was to see his life, but it was past and he had no need for that.

A week after the death of the violinist who could not speak, Father Trelew died. The bishops in New York sent a militant priest who had been embarrassing them to fill his place in Arizona. He died in late afternoon. It had been raining. He knew from years before in his student days that there is a special name for raindrops in Rome because they are often so big, but he could not remember it. He was admiring the light coming off the wet buildings, and he was calm, listening to the wash of the rain. The bushes in the garden glistened with drops, and when someone went by and hit them the water flew off like water off a vibrating dog. Streams of warm water coursed

down the gray stone streets of the mountain—or
hill—of the hospital. All across Rome flocks of pigeons
were seeking the rays of sun, which came from holes
in the clouds, and they flew in great masses, looking
for light that quickly vanished with new configura-
tions of the dark sky. Father Trelew listened to the
work of the rain, to the wash of the rain, and to a car
going through a puddle. The water is warm, the
blood of the earth. He was a man resting for the afternoon in his chair. Warm breezes thick with invisible
mist moved his white gauze curtains, and he faced
the wind. He turned his head to it and breathed it
in.

Then it seemed again as if there were an earthquake. For an instant he imagined that lightning had
hit him, for his vision had flashed white at first, but
then he knew, and when the bolts kept on coming
he knew he was dying and he became very excited.

He tried to think of the girl he had once loved—of
her face, of the heat and their well-being—but he
could not do it. He had not enough time. He realized
that dying takes away time, and that is all, and he was
dying when fear gripped him and his mouth dropped
open in its customary manner. He had planned to die
with a vision, but there was no vision. The rain had
stopped, and the water ceased to flow as rapidly inside the gutters. He noticed that. The walls seemed
to him a very dark olive green instead of tan. His
mouth hung open, but he raised himself in his chair
of a sudden and said, "Damn you, shut, damn it!" and
it did shut and he was so surprised that he smiled and
his eyes came alive. It seemed to him that he was a
new man, that he was no longer a priest, no longer

Michael Trelew. He was only sorry that they would bury him as Michael Trelew, Priest. He had gone out of those doors.

He lived that way for the short span of time between the lighting of his eyes and the entrance of a priest who was rushing in the door to administer last rites. Father Trelew saw the priest through the corner of his eye, but by the time he would have had full view he was dead. The last thing he thought was how beautiful the summer rain in Rome—and he died, and he died with great courage.

Katherine Comes to Yellow Sky

Like a French balloonist who rides above in the clear silence slowly turning in his wicker basket, Katherine rode rapidly forward on a steady-moving train. It glided down depressions and crested hills, white smoke issuing lariat-like from the funnel, but mostly it was committed to the straightness of the path, the single track, the good open way. And as an engine well loved, the locomotive ran down the rails like a horse with a rider.

Passengers sat mainly in silence, not taking one another for granted but rather deeply respectful, for they were unacquainted and there was not the familiarity of one type crossing another. From each could come the unseen, perhaps a strange resolve or stranger ability. Like athletes before a match, they had high mutual regard so that as the day passed from morning to noon each man or woman kept to windows.

Katherine too stared out the imperfect glass ahead at softly glowing grasslands, yellow seas of wheat, seas of wildflowers, and June lilies, and at the dark mountains which were always visible in one direction or another. Having neglected to get a book out of her luggage she could only look, and attempt thoughts and variations. At first it was taking off her thin gold glasses and closing the good left eye so that she could blur the deep permanent colors. This she did, but saw an old man staring at her and at the way she tilted her head and set her mouth as if waiting for an answer she would never believe. She looked daft when she did that or as if she had some kind of rare nerve dance. Back went the glasses and for a while she stared straight and dignified directly into the distance, this soon giving her the appearance of a gorgeous lunatic. She wore a white dress with high white shoes, and an enormous wide-brimmed hat, which although it glowed as fiercely as the face of a glacier was modified in its absoluteness by the buttercup haze of a yellow saffron band. Her hair was a long bright auburn tied back, and her eyes a striking green, as hazy as the saffron glow and as cool as a spring in the mountains, and if it were not that way the burn of freckles on her face might have consumed her, for they gave this girl a hot and sun-colored redness even in the stillest of white winters and a youth that carried her well into age. The daughter of an Irish quarry worker and a Dublin Jewess, she was taken when small enough to be nicknamed "Carroty" from the west of England to Boston and then to Quincy, where her father became a foreman on a new opening in the granite quarry and her mother took up work in a textile mill. Katherine herself went to normal school, escaping lovers because she was wedded to a dream landscape, and although many sought her she was faithful to a vision of clouds and yellow sky far off to the West in unsettled territories. And she passed quickly from the society of the normal school to the company of a solitary idea. Convinced of new worlds her existence was animated in such a way that she had no answers, not a one, but believed incessantly in what she imagined.

She had read all her life of the openness of the West, of its red rivers and plains leafed in neutral in-breathing gold, of the miraculous Indians and the Rockies, which were mountains of mist that formed and unformed dreams so fast as to confuse even the youngest of dreamers. And strangely enough these substanceless dreams, these short electric pictures, these confused but royally intense sketches, gradually gave to her a strength, practicality, and understanding which many a substantial man would never have. Her vindication, almost God-promised, was as clear as the excellent sea air, or the deep blue pools which in summer formed at the bottom of the quarries, to her father's chagrin. Her father, whose strength had equaled the beauty of her mother, had seen in her very early what he himself had lost, and unlike many fathers he had no envy. He was too good for that. He loved her too much. He saw himself as a stone arch, unbending, sheltering around his wife and daughter, to keep them safe and await the day when his daughter could soar on her visions and be settled.

Katherine, a dreamer, was not hard but tender,

and when her parents died one following the other in a general epidemic she was wild. Just to be in Quincy, as gray as a man's suit, afflicted with ice and dark winds, a shabby collection of boards amidst scrub trees like the coat of a dying mare, made her sad in a way which does no good and leads to dead ends and contemptible unbelieving. One day in winter she thought she saw her father standing by her mother, who was gentle and strong and had been the first to die. Her father held a sledgehammer, of the finest wood and with a shining gold head. He said, "I shall free you all," and went to the base of the quarry where he smashed the cast-iron braces and beams which held the rock. The iron rang like a thousand bells and black pieces shattered over the quarry, ringing the pools and echoing off the high walls. And her father continued until every chain was severed and every brace broken, until all metal and all the past were smashed, buried in the clear pools. Free air circulated away from its bounds and the muscular father said to her, a little out of breath but with as good a red color as he had had on the finest days of summer, he said, "Katherine, Katherine, my Carroty, we too have had it with this place. We are not permanently rooted here, and you must go away. I have smashed these bonds, and this I did for you. Pile your hair, tie it firmly, and find a new place."

This she did, about a year later, and headed West, for there she sensed something which would give her the moments she wanted before her death, moments of full cognizance and dream vision, the red roses of her life and its humor. It was good to abandon Quincy and its quarry.

She set her hat at an angle, trying to frame the light blue mountain ranges. The tracks threw up dust and she eyed steam from the locomotive. These billowing clouds became captions for her thoughts, and they centered on Yellow Sky, on a dream quest which had spread to all the people. Yellow Sky. It was still far off.

That night they stopped in Gibson, a town spread across a large rise in the prairie where cattle roads, a flat unnavigable river, and the railroad crossed at angles. Huge yards of seemingly spider-work boards held cattle for boxcar loading, and during the whole of the late spring night, cattle filed past her window in the darkness. Without awakening her assigned roommate, an elderly woman who looked like a tomb, Katherine stepped out of bed and went to the open window. A high wind carried occasional raindrops past the town and out into the vastly promising darkness from which an endless procession of moody steers was filing—giant animals intent upon moving to their slaughter—to feed the distant cities. She had seen the land-seas of wheat and flowers and from them came these steers, an abundance which kept her awake the rest of the night wide-eyed, waiting for the hoofbeats and dust and drovers' calls to stop, but when morning found her tears were in her eyes as she stared at the clouds of sparkling dust. From where did they come, constantly, without even the slightest break? The land beyond was empty except for storm and mountains, and yet from there the night had been filled with a power so great it drew a shaking tense silence, a joyous fright. The endless power was born somewhere out near Yellow Sky, and

Katherine couldn't sleep because she was headed there, as surely and certainly as the warm steel track, or the confident horsemen who often appeared alongside to race the train.

Leaving Gibson, they skirted the wide river and crossed a road on which thousands of cattle were backed up for miles; in the distance they were as even a brown as the drovers' felt hats. For scores of miles the landscape was the same, a rolling plain which looked like masses of brown whales, dotted flowers, banks of lilies, and grasses. The train's exact and faithful forward motion led her to expect something ahead at all moments, and although there was nothing save the glittering May landscape, the convincing direction became in itself more than enough to hold her, and hold her it did, as had her realization of the night power in and around Gibson. She was held fast, but no more than anyone on the train, no more than farmers, fencemen, or drovers outside who were passed by and left to work amid their own silence and claimed lands, no more than boys in Gibson who prodded cattle with dry white cotton-willow sticks, or distant horsemen on a ridge, galloping only to disappear, although leaving the surety of their gallop impressed upon the passengers. A detachment of pony soldiers, '75 blue, rode two by two on a wagon track, swords and buckles shining. They did not always know what they did, but by God they did it, as it was inevitable. Had she not lived her life in grayness and seen the bright only by fantasy? Did she not as the daughter of a man deserve these rich lands which had been declared ready and were being gathered in the arms of those who had come from such long ways away? Yellow Sky was in the mountains, up high, beyond the timberline which was like a skirt. The air was as thin as shell and pearl bright as the lakes and plummeting black-rock streams. She would stop in Yellow Sky but others would pass right on, and yet others right down to the broken beaches of the Pacific. This young impressionable girl alone on the cool wicker-weave seat of a shady railroad car moving out West could not be stopped. The colors in her were bound for Yellow Sky.

At about six in the morning the tired train halted in a cool saddle of the mountains just above the tree-line. Men began to carry wood from enormous stock-piles along the track and load it on the coaler. A wooden trough was lowered from a cable-bound bar-rel tank and mountain water fell into the blackened holds of the locomotive, dribbling, spraying, and steaming from valves of nickel and steel, hissing like a swarm of locusts in the convoluted boilers. The steam from the locomotive's gaskets mingled with the early morning mist, low clouds which hid white gold-flecked mountains of sunrise. The peaks had begun to shine many hours before, and after sunset they would shine even though the night was black, the price for this advanced and delayed burnishing of the mountains being shade and darkness at the ex-treme hours. Those who lived in that place stared each day in special communication at the shining crowns all about them. The man who had charge of the railroad depot was tall and wore hobnailed boots which awakened passengers as he walked on top of the cars. His boots also awakened his children, a little

bear-faced boy and two fat little girls happy to have
only their own thousands of private jokes.

The one hundred or so people in the town were
miners, bridge workers, and railroad men who rode
small mounted donkey engines up and down the
passes securing faulted track and removing obstruc-
tions. There were always bridges to build, sometimes
of several yards, sometimes of a quarter of a mile, because it was ravine country, rocky, high, indifferent
to smooth-trafficking men and natural only to birds
such as eagles, hawks, crows, and falcons—mountain
birds with eyes of wondrous and staggering capabili-
ties. Sharp as a ten-foot glass, they still could not see
veins of silver spread variously throughout the ravines and deep into rock where only men could go,
and by great effort. The trackers held the land down
by use of iron bands, the bridgemen smoothed it, and
the miners pierced it—as if they were hunters and
it a mammoth, succumbing to their studied attack.

The attack was not studied but passionate, and not
of greed alone. At each days' end the bridgemen, the
railroadmen, the miners looked at the land in the
quiet time when the mountains shone softly like lanterns into the dark valley, and they saw that it was
not damaged. Work as they did, the peaks were high,
the streams excellently fresh, the pastures rich, their
iron and wood, their fences and track all but invisible
due to the greatness of the land. This, as much as anything else, made them love it. It was invincible and
so beckoned, challenging them to make their mark.
Impossible, they said when they looked up, for the
sky was as blue as a pure packet of indigo, and it
reached into deep unconquerable heaven.

The conductor (who had warned Katherine to be careful of sparks—prompting her to say that it was impossible to be careful of sparks) roused her from a fitful, watery-eyed, straight-backed, sitting-up, night never ends sleep and she with the rest of the passengers stepped into a mountain village where they were served tea and rolls. Katherine stood quietly at yet another window, this in the depot, and she saw in the distance the lantern mountains glowing gold in all directions, catching the future sun. There, and just then did she realize, was the source of the power she had sensed days before. This time it was realization which struck her, not revelation, and there were no tears or risings within. She simply realized in the deadest and most sober of moments that in those mountains was the source, glancing off high lighted rock faces where no man could ever go, split into rivers eastward and westward running in little fingers to every part of the land, to the oceans where it blended with the newly turned sea foam and sun.

As the sun became stronger, but still not visible, they re-embarked onto the train. When Katherine approached the three-stepped iron stand, the conductor offered her his hand. She wondered why, thinking that perhaps he was going to help her up, something he did not do. But he shook her hand, and barred her way. Why? she said, and then he pointed to her luggage—leather cases and white canvas duffels—and when she still did not understand, to the mountains with golden light like the warm light from a candle. She was struck dumb. The train began to pull away, conductor and all, with a vast exhalation of white steam, and he said to the stunned girl what she already knew, "This is Yellow Sky." As the train vanished she could think only of her father, her mother, and the gray oceans in between. Oceans in between, their lights had lasted, and she had found her way. It came in a flood, and she shuddered. Oceans in between. It was an end. It was a beginning. Katherine had come to Yellow Sky.

Elisha Hospital

They are building a new wing, but nevertheless it is quiet. On instructions from the contractor the men work slowly, almost silently. With each board or frame it is as if a decision must be made: shall we tighten this, or shall we let it rest? The old men with shirts wrapped around their heads inevitably continue, although one has the impression that perhaps someday they simply will not work and instead lean on their trowels or sit on the sacks of concrete. At the rate they work, it is hard to tell if they are building or tearing down.

It is the same with us, I suppose, when we treat a dying patient. Like the old Iraqi Jews who pour the cement, we, too, must decide whether or not to tighten our patient's dying frame or just to let it dissolve and run away on the light blue air.

Blue is the predominant color at Elisha. It is seen everywhere out the big windows, from their tops to their bottoms, because we are on the summit of a hill—better to say mountain, although I hesitate to call anything a mountain unless it is capped with snow. Most windows look north; the ease of the light is inescapable; a soft clear altitude of blue air flees from all sides. Ships at sea, like small precision engines enameled in red and orange and black, move across a glass of blue. Passengers in a German dirigible would have had it no better than patients here. It is true they could move from place to place, but at Elisha we have no vibration—not even from the construction. Except for the souls that die within, it is a perfect environment.

It is in this hospital that I met my wife. On chill November evenings we made tea in the laboratory, which overlooks the Hadar; the bright orange flame of a Bunsen burner and the tea in a glass beaker made the dark cold and hissing respiratory winds outside less terrible. I remember well staring at a large desk calendar underneath a fluorescent light, trying to fix the time and feeling permanently. I did. It was November 15, 1965, and it was ten o'clock. As I have said, the wind was whistling outside and it was dark and we were in love. And the clear light and sounds nearly matched our excitement. We spoke of Switzerland, and California, and Paris, and we have been to those places and we have been back.

We had then grave aspirations, as doctors might. We have achieved some of them, others have been whittled away by the world. We have not been bent by great events so that we are something other than ourselves, with an enemy within. On the contrary, we have been lucky. I have been in war but not in the thick of it. I have been in upheaval but not in the thick of it. I have never been concerned with governments, one way or another, because one way or another they have never been much concerned with me.

The first of this September marked the opening of school. Even I shared the excitement of the new year. As I walked to the hospital I passed a high school, the courtyard of which was jammed with noisy foolish students from whom—contrary to the popular assumption—one should not learn but rather take revival. A beautiful young girl reminded me of my wife and of the autumn when we met. The trees were rustling and it was cool in the shade, and I left as she was blushing because I had stared intently.

I was in a good mood; it was my day in the month solely for the medical library, and there is no better work than to sit there and read. But on my way upstairs I wanted to stop in at X-ray, so I began walking down the corridor, where windows of bright blue are one wall and silver doors and yellow benches are are the other. Outside the operating rooms was a young man of about twenty-five and his girl child. He was tall and slim, with dark hair and very dark skin. Not strangely—it was, after all, at Elisha above the sea and hills—he was wearing a bright and fine blue shirt. His daughter, a child like many I have seen, was tiny and beautiful. She had grown out of infancy, but one had to look twice to make certain. Like her father she had dark hair and dark skin. I judged that they had been at the beach in August, for she was almost a chocolate color, the whites of her eyes and the loose white gown in which she was enwrapped contrasting to make a luminescence.

I remembered this child. I had heard that she was very sick and did not have much chance to live. I had not given it thought. It would be too hard to give thought to such things all the time. She had received anesthesia and was busy losing consciousness, perhaps for the last time, while her father held her in his arms, rocked her, put her little head next to his face, and gathered in her legs. He was worried that perhaps the anesthesia was not working, and as I was passing he looked at me.

"She is falling asleep?" he said.

"Yes," I said. "I can see that it won't be long." I put my hands in my pockets and stood as if to talk, for there was no one else there and I was almost sure of the outcome. He held her very closely—I have never seen a man as tender with a child—until she was fast asleep and a gowned and masked operating-room nurse came through swinging doors to take the child and carry her within.

Nothing could be said, so I said, "You are a new immigrant?" since it was evident from his speech.

"Yes," he said.

"From where?" although that was also evident.

"From Russia—Kiev," he replied, a little more at ease. "I was to be a curator of arts at the museum, and then . . ." He raised his arms and smiled. "And then . . ."

"And what do you do here?"

"I work as an artist commercial, but soon I am going to study at the university, when my wife comes. She is still in Kiev."

I was reluctant to leave him alone. At such times quiet institutions are murderous, but I had to do my reading. "Look," I said, "these things can be difficult. If there is anything I can do to help, anything at all for whatever reason . . . If you need something, or just to talk—you know? I will be in the library, upstairs," and I pointed. I touched him on the shoulder and left quickly.

I spent that day in the library. Later in the evening when it was dark, I walked bleary-eyed past the empty yellow bench where he had been sitting. His lighter and cigarettes were there. I dared not learn the outcome. A warm light met the dark blue of the windows, then almost black, and I left Elisha Hospital, thinking of my wife and sons and how history had left me in peace. A dark September rain began to fall, as one seldom sees it fall in Haifa.

End of the Line

In Sicily one always finds precedent. The barber cuts hair according to precedent, flies land according to custom, a route is taken because it was taken before, and although a certain crop is unprofitable it may be cultivated for years on end simply because of tradition.

For example, in the town of Nuovo Fantasio, pronounced in the old way with the stress upon the "i," there is a date orchard belonging to the family Della Mercedi. It is an old, high orchard with thick trees nearly seventy-five feet before the crown. It is a square with ninety trees to a side, but only eight thousand all together, because in the center is a luxurious shaded garden built at the sacrifice of one-hundred trees, intimate, for it is a Roman square of ten trees on each side, and enormous for the very fact that it displaces one-hundred massive trunks. This orchard was planted by a Caliph who genuinely

believed Sicily to be an outcropping of North Africa.
For a thousand years the trees grew, died, and left
a stream of child trees providing an income of heavy
dates for many families of Muslims, Spanish, Nor-
mans, and lastly the Della Mercedi, who followed
their line somehow back to Spain but could not be
sure.

The orchard was not fertile, and had not been for
quite some time. At the tops of date palms are long
sharp spears, modified leaves which have become
weapons against the birds in a million generations of
fighting and steadfastness while the swordlike green-
ery rolled itself into spikes. All good things come
from a struggle, even the simple fruit of a date palm,
from a struggle of planting, growing, and staying. A
tree will only be fertile if much labor is expended in
making it so, and for years there had not been
enough labor in Sicily, at least not there. More than
half the people had left for America, and after the
war for northern Europe, where they worked in factories and sent home money to those who remained.
The government built a textile mill and opened a
new cut in the marble quarry, so that whatever laborers there were had much better work to do than
climbing high ladders which came to narrow points
so they could be positioned around the spikes, so that
the fruit could be reached and regenerated.

Some of the fruit had by chance blackened into
ripeness but most was red and unfertile, a terra-cotta
color which seemed to satirically reflect the sun's afternoon blazing. There were so many crows with no
one to chase them away by day that the noise from
their wings was like an express train or the Sirocco.

The earth was sulfurous, or at least smelled so, and the mountains were a pale yellow and white.

When the sun set, a special patina of silver and green traced itself across the orchard, in between the tall thorn-tressed trees. The roof of the sky, having been white hot, cooled, enabling the crows to ride upward on rivers of yellowed and cold sea air.

Signora Della Mercedi, and her son Paolo, were the two Della Mercedi left to claim the land. Her husband had died long before, so that she had forgotten even what it was like to wear anything but black. A son, her best son, had been killed in the war. His name was Giorgio, the father's hope, for he was strong and manly even when a boy. There was one other son, Thomaso, a wretch, a gourmand who lived, or rather ate, in Rome. He spent, borrowed, gambled, and ate. He had control of the revenues from the land, what revenues there were, an unfortunate accident due to the fact that he was the eldest surviving son and his mother had never been taught to read. Paolo was confined to a wheelchair, and spent his time listening to a giant German short-wave set bequeathed to him by his father. At least he was not like his brother Thomaso, who, to his mother's complete incredulity, loved only men.

There were so many problems now for Signora Della Mercedi as she approached her old age. Government people came from Palermo to demand taxes which had not been paid. The house was in terrible disrepair. Servants (there were two, always changing) would go to the town with enough money for some meat, some cheese, and bread, and come back with bread, which became that night's dinner.

She was silent, for she did not really care what she ate. The problems were like crows, cowardly and unimportant when alone, but bold and terrible in their thousands.

Once her husband had taken her into the date orchard in the evening. They were young, their children still infants, and the trees producing like factories. He was a big man who ate mainly meat, whiskey, and pastry, and he was a rich man who liked to gamble and have expensive things like German radios and a Bugatti motor car. He screamed suddenly with great power, "Zapata!", and the noise of ten thousand wings rose skyward from the thick dark palms, making her leap into his arms for she was truly frightened.

He was an aristocrat, a baron of lands which had been his whole life and his father's too. When he was a small child he had looked up at the tall trees and seen men high in the air working at the fertilization. There were no more real titles, and there would not have been for the Della Mercedi anyway, but there could still be men like her husband, men with a singularity of purpose refined as in a fire. She thought that there must be always true aristocrats in fact and privilege, so that everyone might enjoy the pretense—for everyone does. The baron had been a kind man, expert in plant genetics, fond of Cézanne (having several reproductions), and above all, committed to staying in Sicily even though all his brothers and so many others had left. Why? He didn't know, but to stay against all odds was dramatic and noble, the real source of his nobility, his fight.

Things went on in Rome about which she had

heard and not even vaguely comprehended. She could see from the shrine on top of the mountain where she went in summer in July on the Feast of St. Ann tremendous long ships which passed into and out of sight within minutes. She knew the world was changing, but all of its motion was just beyond the horizon, something to be seen with a sideways glance. And therefore she had decided to stay on her lands, though they might be impoverished and dry, though the government might appropriate them year by year decree by decree as was done when taxes went unpaid, though her sons did not have and would not have sons of their own.

Without fail, she went every evening at dusk to the Roman Garden, which had become choked with weeds and grass, where her husband had yelled. "Zapata!" forty years before. She would bring with her a stick. After coming up the small hill she stood breathless in the half light, unafraid and alone, and thought of her husband and his wish not to leave the land. She had no grandsons, and that was bitter fruit, but as if to ward off the crows circling above she said, "Hail Mary full of grace, the Lord is with Thee. Blessed art Thou among women, and blessed is the fruit of Thy womb, Jesus. Holy Mary, mother of God, pray for us sinners now and at the hour of our death."

And then she banged the thick trunk of a palm, yelling "Zapata! Zapata!", with her eyes fiercely staring at the black cloud of birds fleeing upwards.

The Legitimacy of Medium Beauty

In beginning autumn there is a wind which comes on high clear days and grips the trees, drawing them out and shaking them beyond several of their breaths, while their leaves rattle like a wind in themselves and seem like jewels or green water. These winds are chainwinds, never ceasing, and on those days they scourge all the land and water with peace and clarity and sun and coolness. In Atlanta they had come only in the late fall and sometimes in the summer when the heat broke and the clearness seemed to be shimmering in itself. But here south of San Francisco, in mountains where there are redwoods and low high altitudes and abandoned cabins abandoned only recently but never so, and always with damp dark floorboards and a mattress wet on its springs when you enter into the darkness from the dark black stream and its numb moving waters, and the brown pine needles and black pieces of earth that stick on the feet when you step carefully on the porch—here that jeweled chain of air moved way up the tops of trees, far above the gloom of rays and roots and fallen trees. And when she looked up at the blue through the red wood she saw the clouds moving like ghosts and their horses, making the upper branches shudder and hiss. She often wandered here, and to the south in the valley, and evening found her driving back into San Francisco, ruddy and sad but not sad enough to be unhappy.

She was Mary from Atlanta, who thought in wide circles about porches and the past and small towns in summer—facts and memories of detail which transfixed her at the wheel of her open car and made her arms shake and her back cold, although these things were not remarkable, and neither was her life. Neither was her life, a life of love although she did not know for what, unless it was for small pictures which occurred to her or which she saw in quiet moments alone staring at the whiteness of the castled city or across the Bay to reddened mountains and leonine hills with yellowed brush tumbling from their sides.

The phone was green, the windows wide, the floor waxed and yellowed wood, her dress a print by Marimekko, liquor on a glass cart, cuttingboards in the kitchen, twelve bottles of wine, much Lucite such as blocks with photographs embedded and an end table, a bed high enough off the floor to kill, an old dresser, high rent, magazines and a bookshelf full of women novels which cannot ever be read again because they are gossip, dependent on plot and sequence rather than the static truth, many memories of men, in the beginning at least, who had stayed but none to let her in. All seemed too eager or too serious, too capable, or too hard. Perhaps it was because she herself put them off by speaking hard and being skeptical, as if she assumed they had no memories and could think and act only like modern furniture. And then the liquor would start to flow. Liquor is magic for furniture, but afterwards she could think only of getting them out and jumping into the bath. One morning an especially timid one tiptoed into the kitchen and poured himself a glass of orange juice over ice. While reading her copy of that month's *Vogue* he was startled so by ice shifting in the glass that he jumped back, knocking himself unconscious against a wall. Once there was one so large and dumb that he drew himself a tub of water, stepped in, and displaced it. One was an accountant, one a lobster executive, and one an actor who stood naked.

But furniture, no matter how droll, was furniture, if she could be carried at a mite's breath to a childhood carnival, the American Legion, hardened women at shooting galleries, soldiers and their wives with angular eyes and almond glasses, late night heat and flashing lights at the gray cotton sky, and the screen door during a carried half sleep shutting until another day and mirages on the sand-colored roads.

Now she was large—not fat, but big-boned with an upturned nose and pores that could be seen too well in the magnifying mirror. She looked like her mother, whom she had never thought pretty, but it seemed unnecessary for her mother to be that way when the little girl Mary had a face which was small and smooth as a chestnut and could be clasped in her father's hand in riotous fun.

That little fine face was now large, and she imagined that her head alone weighed as much as the little girl she once was. But she was quick enough not to be bound to that, and she was not. It was something, just something. No special state or time or thought but only the occasional gripped her sense of herself.

San Francisco has hills. She lived clean on one of them, and enjoyed good climate. She was lovely but all around her would suffice. She was lovely but she found herself growing out of it, and getting older to where she would have to find for herself a sustaining power. Her dreams were dead, memories not enough, she felt nought for God, and she had no passion. But a deep and beautiful sadness reigned, so that San Francisco moved slowly like a swan, and she drew from everything she saw enough to make her life a deep cool color, a medium beauty, that full wind which made the trees shudder, and draw breath, and seem like green water.

The Home Front

Before the Battle of the Wood could get itself going, most of early June had passed. Originally headquarters had intended the confrontation to begin on 1 June exactly. But messages between commanders had been late in coming, and supplies were delayed on the way to the front. This was because the messengers and mule drivers, farm boys, took their time in crossing the countryside of new summer. Often an entire supply train—a hundred, perhaps two or three hundred caissons—would pull off the road onto the green so drivers and guards could swim in the clean, swirling waters of a little river. Messengers dangled along the ridges walking their horses, passing slowly through the leafy fringe and perfect climate. There was no galloping along the white roads. Obsessions about buttoning brass buttons had passed, all the young men in the army were red and tanned the beautiful color of summer's first sun, and it seemed to each man that his haircut was perfect and his clothes in perfect press. There was a blaze then, but for the cool evenings, and the army moving in great thin lines through the rich green from one place to another was like a fresh blue wake.

Of the many soldiers from McLean, Virginia, was one who came to be known as Jack, and then for some reason as either Jack Japan or The Glass. In Virginia in this time of summer he had often walked along the stagnant curve of the river to the war cemetery where he lay in quiet among white flags and lilies. But he had not been nearly as alive as he was now before the Battle of the Wood, seemingly all-seeing and as excited as the thrushing of the overhead branches. Beginning summer was always good, but never had he felt so well his life and its every moment: riding in a truck with two rows of fellow soldiers, walking to the river and just standing there watching, mounting a horse and seeing the saddle close up as his body bent like a complex machine designed to make quick curves, being in the shade, eating in the afternoon when it was cooler, just arising and facing everything. They all knew they were on the eve of a large offensive. There had been a fine peace for too long. When summer burst it seemed only to verify great change. They were afraid. Carrion had survived the fall because it had been cold and dry, and then the winter, and then spring. Where the animal had settled, a paste of mud and dust had shielded it, and the cold evenings helped, too. But by June carrion infected the woods and the sides of the roads. The countryside was thick in places with the natural smell of death, just the death

of squirrels and other small hunted animals, but it
was enough to signal the men of a waiting army.

Orders came at intervals, so that Jack spent his
time marching into the stream of other columns and
making many new camps, one more beautiful than
another. Then one day an order came by way of a
messenger with a dark face and black saber-
mustache. This man was no boy, and it appeared,
from his bearing and the way he thrived on a quick
gallop and the sight of the road before him and from
his black belts crossing the spring coat of the uniform, that he was part of a real war and not just the
uneasy dream before a true shattering battle. He had
passed through the camp smiling, carrying in his
hand a white paper requesting of the commander
half a hundred men with shovels and full packs to be
on burial detail for one-quarter of one unimportant
flank. Burial detail struck the half a hundred as provi-
dential and yet very unlucky. Unless there were a
breakthrough by enemy cavalry and long and terrible sweeps, they would be safe. The job was not good
and there was no chance of seeing the battle and surviving it so that they might have the particular ela-
tion which comes from getting through and the privilege of saying to women that they had been there.
Burial detail cut out all but the worst of liars from tav-
ern stories, and made soldiery impossible for them
ever again. But burial detail it was to be, so they
formed their ranks, which broke quickly when it was
discovered that there were shovels only for a few.
Everyone ran off in a different direction to search the
barns and boarded-up houses, hoping to come upon
a young girl, or a wife, bathing naked in a river or

lying in the sun with only a thin sheet, trying to look beautiful and get the golden hair to shine. Jack thought how nice the women of Virginia looked in the light of candles after they had been in the sun all day working or just staying by the river. But they found no women at all, only shovels in such great number that they left many behind with comrades whom they hoped with all their hearts not to see during the battle. They marched back into the quiet country whence they had come and where they saw no cannon or troops, or even telegraph lines.

They said little, preferring to walk quietly and take in the sun, which during the afternoon stared right in their faces as they marched below great flourient oaks and trees with blooming flowers. Then they came to a wide field. On the northern half of a small green prairie were hundreds of dressing stations, round white tents in orderly rows. They looked like mushrooms. And they were far away, so that it was hard to make out the red crosses. The burial detail entered the field from the east and walked away from the tents to a row of straight trees in the south to set up camp. Behind these trees was a smaller field of about an acre. They discovered that the heavy brush bordering it on three sides was laden with blackberries and songbirds, and hives of bees. It took only a few hours to pitch ten tents, get a good supply of wood, find water, and have an inspection. Their uniforms were clean and they had eaten. Given the afternoon off, some went into the brush to brave the bees and gather blackberries for themselves and for the cook, who had the other things for a pie but lacked a filling. Some went to a small stream and, even though it was too shallow for swimming, let the water course over them while they looked up at the pines on the steep bank. Jack Japan, The Glass, filled a bag with pine needles and he and some others kicked it around the field where the graves would be.

They had only to wait. After a short cold dinner they drank their coffee and became aware of the nurses. Across the field they could see nurses in almost glowing white making quick lines from tent to tent. The lieutenant used his telescope to report that women near the fires were staring downfield at the opposing ranks of flame. On both sides of the meadow, hands went up to fix hair and straighten collars. Then, perhaps because it was wartime, and they had also been there first, about a hundred of the nurses began to walk slowly into the dark. They came from all along the line, two or three carrying lanterns which showed the gentle night breeze. At the gravediggers' it was as if an enemy army were converging. The men felt frightened at being still, so a number of them set out for the middle, and after a little while the rest followed. They met, and strolled back to the dressing stations in a lighthearted manner, as if they were not a contingent of nurses and gravediggers but just young men and young women at a June ball. There was easy laughing of the kind when people do not know one another and yet want to. Billy Fair took his five-stringed banjo from a black case he had been carrying strapped to his back like a rifle, and he played for a long time and put everyone at ease. They wished they had some wine, but there was none. Although many were complimented by them, no one could see the uniforms—just the faces of those across the fires. For years they had all worn bits and pieces of uniforms from surplus, and had craved them. But in full dress with real insignia they felt a good deal less romantic. A girl imagined herself in a white gown, and a boy there wanted to be wearing a fine dark suit with a white flower. Beyond the fires, moon-whitened grass touched like a girl's hand to music in all directions because of the night breeze.

The nurses had little to do, for the battle had not started, and soon there was a free exchange with the burial detail, and swimming and Field Day games. They took walks into the forest where they saw deer and herons, where everything was hot and nature fast music moving to excite them. Jack took up with a French Canadian nurse named Montay, who swam with him and told him that the herons in the small lake were not loons. He hardly knew her for she and he shared a gloss as if in a dream, something they didn't mind at all, because they could dream breakers out in the field—so unreal was his life, the life of a conscripted soldier in an enormous field where the men were served blackberry pies and sunburned nurses glided across in evening to sit by the fires and the men they found, who found them, too.

One day a doctor walked across the field to speak with the tall lieutenant. In his clean white tunic the doctor pointed to the small field and indicated how he wanted the graves. He wanted five pits: thirty feet long, ten feet wide, and eight feet deep. He advised them to start right away, because he had heard that the offensive was due to begin any time. Since they faced a well-fortified enemy, it was necessary to prepare for heavy casualties. The graves would take three hundred, good enough for the first few days at least. Quickly they began to dig, ten to a grave, and the lieutenant did not supervise but removed his tunic and worked beside the men. Nor was there any military discipline, for they thought of themselves as gravediggers, and what a world it would be if gravediggers were disciplined. Soldiering for them was already dead and worn. They looked fine though, in striped military pants with suspenders hanging down their thighs. It took them two days of digging in silence to finish, for in some places the ground was hard.

Then a messenger galloped into the dressing station and fires were lit in preparation for the wounded, who arrived within a few hours. During the first night Jack lay on his blanket and watched the many fires and lanterns across the field. Ambulances came often, shining their lights on the tents. There were many fires; it became hot in the nights, and he wondered if Nurse Montay, whom he hardly knew and whom he missed though she was just on the other side of the enameled green, was sweating by the night fires as she worked.

In the daytime the first dead were brought on hideous blood-soaked stretchers. The men were white, and Jack lowered them without shrouds into the graves. At night he stared at the fires, and then at the great overflowing masses of high white stars above him in untangled black. They trailed the sky and brought morning. He made more graves, did not bother to wash, and found that his clothes were filthy. Every day the ambulances became more numerous. The battle had swung their way. It was hot, and it got hotter, and they had no beer.

On their last evening there, when graves covered the small clearing, as if in a dream a nurse rode up on a sweaty brown mare. The mare's saddle and blanket were soaked into blackness and the nurse was covered with layers of mud and dust which made her clothes and face the telling pea-green color of an army road. Her white uniform and its blue, chevron-shaped, gently falling collar were splattered up to her hair, which was golden and had retained its sheen. The gravediggers gathered around her; one held the bridle of her horse and comforted it, for it was in profound exhaustion. The silent men could see that she was selfless, that she had been battered, and that she had come from the front, where they knew the machines were working which sent them their dead. She had retained her beauty though she was gray and colorless but for her hair. Her mouth was especially exquisite and her teeth white. It was painful pleasure to watch her speak.

"Is there anything we can do?" said Jack after a long silence, and they all waited for her answer.

"Yes," she said, "yes . . ."

"Tell us," said another soldier.

"I am looking for my husband. He was on the line, and then he was wounded and they brought him to my dressing station. He had influenza as well. I was gone for just a little while, but when I returned his bed was empty. I was wondering," she said, "I was wondering . . ." And then she cast her eyes level to the acre of buried dead and stared for a long time, a long, long time, during which there was silence and they could hear the steady blows of an ax across the field. Fires burned to her left and to her right, the horse was no longer winded and she herself seemed to sit straight as an officer.

One of the men took off his hat, and gesturing toward the graves, looked downward as if in shame and said, "These are mass graves, ma'am."

As if they had never existed she pulled her horse around, spurred it, and went out toward the road. The men remembered only that she had been high above them and that her expression had been hard.

The following morning, when they had buried more than a thousand men, the cook announced that his blackberry wine although sweet and young was ready to drink. It was very intoxicating. Jack had learned to distinguish the men he buried. Some he could see were killed by machine gun fire, some by shrapnel, some by disease. Some were officers, some had been dead a long time, some looked like people he knew, and some even looked like himself.

They drank wine because there was no breakfast, and they became extremely drunk. A dead soldier in blue and red was entrusted to Jack, who began to talk to him. He spoke to him as if he were alive, and as if the body were a drunken friend he carried him to a grave and dumped him in saying, "In you go."

Digging was not so easy with the wine, but he worked hard, smashing his shovel fiercely and ineffectively at the ground by the field's edge where there were rocks, since it had gone unplowed in peacetime. Every few minutes the cook came around with a huge bottle and poured wine into the men and the graves.

As they were covering the last grave, and reluctant to start another, they noticed that the white tents were folding. An endless line of ambulances came to take away the wounded. In less than an hour everyone from the other side of the field was gone. There was no smoke—no fires either. The gravediggers were astonished. They did not fear that the enemy would close in, because they had heard that he had been defeated. They had won.

In their drunkenness they could think of nothing to do but pat down the earth of the twelve raised mounds in the small field. They packed it down with their feet after they had finished the last of the wine. They went back and forth over the clay until clouds of dust arose in the sun, which had sunk low and become all red. The wine was gone, and so were the nurses; the graves were packed down. Some soldiers went to bathe in the river and wash their clothes. Some, like Jack, went to different parts of the field, where in the smoky red evening of what had been a clear yellow day they threw themselves down on the grass and awakened much later to see no fires, no lanterns, but only the high indifferent stars.

Willis Avenue

If, when I am drunk or sentimental, or prodded by a stupid friend, I think back to the women I have really loved, most of them are covered and hidden by wishes and disappointment. But there is one of whom my memory is clear, and it is strange—she was so unimportant.

She was named Johanna, and I knew her for a summer when I worked in a typewriter-ribbon factory in the Bronx. It was very simple. She sat across from me on the production line all day long, and when either of us lifted our eyes we saw one another. Our job was to put the spools of ribbon in boxes—a very boring job—a job which left our hands automatic, and faces and eyes free so that we spent many days looking and talking. She was not such an attractive girl, and she knew it. These days I don't like beautiful girls so much, anymore. It makes them less able to cry and be sad, and I won't have a girl who cannot cry and be sad.

Now Johanna had a big wide face, and big heavy limbs, although she was not fat by any means, just big. She was in fact bigger than me but she thought like a very delicate woman, and so she moved as if she were little. Although she was not in the least self-conscious about her body (I often saw her breasts as she leaned over to get more boxes and her open shirt came more open), she thought that perhaps she should be, and I could always tell that she was thinking to herself, I have to be more delicate about myself. But she could not be, and the exposure she suffered made her no less attractive to me.

I confess that at first this was not so. She was big and my image of women had been so ideal; I imagined them as princesses and perfectly clean. I thought that perhaps I might sleep with her, understanding that it would not lead to anything. Then I took pity on her for her clumsiness and the way she was impressed by me. I am externally slick, rather handsome, people say. She thought I was beyond her reach; I did too. I took her to lunch, and she blushed under the fan in the little restaurant. The heat of that summer was so intense that it made us both sweat in the shade. She was taken by me and I was therefore not very interested in her. After all she was not very pretty. And every day we sat for eight hours sweating, our legs sometimes touching, across from one another under the inky breeze of the big fan. She looked down so much not because she needed to see to put the spool into the box, but because she was shy, and think, I had told her everything, wanting to make her a sister. She was very unhappy when I told her of the women I thought about that summer. When I first mentioned Nina she looked so sad that I stopped, but later I went on, and I would speak to her of my girls, and I think she cried in the women's dressing room. The other women avoided her and thought she was strange.

We had lunch together every day. All she did was keep still, and laugh with me, and smile when I spoke without thinking. She went home to her mother each afternoon; she spoke well, but she was just not pretty.

In the South Bronx one feels as though one is in the hotter part of Naples or the dull part of the Great Plains. Dirt falls from the air, and the heat, the heat, makes everything, even the iron, wet. And the heat changes people. The people I don't like complain about the heat. Johanna, whom I saw every hour of every day, sitting next to a half-painted column in the skylight light of a hot dirty workroom, did not complain about the heat, but wiped her forehead with her hand now and then and seemed to me very much like myself. She seemed to be me when I was not worried about things, when I was quiet and watching, when I had fallen and could learn and feel, in the heat, the rising heat of that time. Johanna, white-faced and green-eyed, darting-eyed, hands full of ink, wiping her brow with her wrist and getting ink on her wide face anyway. Johanna in the South Bronx in a hot summer when I was stronger and when I thought I would succeed, sat across from me each day. And then I left, and she had to sit there in the same place, and when January came around she was there, accepting whoever sat across from her. I don't think I would have her now, but if she could know that I loved her then more than anything, that I would have married her, loved her, if only I had not been so young, if only I had known myself. Johanna. When she wiped her brow with her wrist she got ink on her face anyway, and she was always smiling.

Elizabeth Ridinoure

When Nathaniel was eighteen and had no place to go he joined the Coast Guard. They sent him to Maine where he served aboard a small cutter in Casco Bay. From day to day his life accelerated in company with white spray from a heaving blue sea gracefully turned back upon itself by a steel cutter, white except for a diagonal red stripe sleeking the bow—the guns white, the rivets the decks the transom the rails and even the sound of the engines white. Nathaniel had been born in a time when everything was expected. Having finished with the greatest war, no one could imagine another so it was lids off in bringing up children. They were raised to seek pleasures and believe myths. When these children were young men they obscenely smashed what they had obscenely believed. They did not understand the time from which they had come, and having let blind men lead them they then turned to the halt to lead them away. Naturally they went no-where, having been taught that only the best of men are leaders. A generation so well treated can be fit only for early death. They were born in war, and those born in war will die in war.

Nathaniel was different. It would be hard indeed to say just how much his cutter pleased him. He was on duty for weeks at a time. In winter the rough sea and generous fog made him silent and content, teaching him that life on earth and the earth itself must rest in darkness, quiet, and shrouds of mist. In winter he learned to navigate by sight and sound pre-cisely, to do dangerous things. He took part in the rescue of a freighter which had run aground. The sailors were Portuguese and African and they looked with special terror at the numbing sea and with won-der at the blue-jacketed Americans whose quarter they had come upon. Standing like a harpooner at the bow of the motorized whaleboat Nathaniel had pulled the frightened wet men in, leaning down far into the air above the sea and lifting each man with a smile. "Hello," he said to each one as he hoisted him up like a baby. The Portuguese and the Africans could not understand how their rescuers could live so happily with so much ice, and arrive on time in a white ship with a red stripe and excellent coffee, as well as radar and guitars. They listened to opera that night, coming on the short wave directly from Milan.

In summer he grew dark and stronger and kept his uniform cleaner for the sake of women on the yachts. Baby girls on the dock watched him coiling lines or painting and asked him questions like: "Why do they put fish in a can?" which he answered and entered in the ship's log. He was good at his work and he loved his ship, the bay, the sea, all the coasts and sandy cliffs, and most importantly his life, which he had suspected since he was a child would end before he was full grown. This was his genuine belief. He was not about to make it happen, and he would even fight the death he serenely knew he was born into, but not wildly. Wild fighting is often good, but in some ages it is simply undignified. So he spent each year as if it were the last, each day in fact, and his powers of observation increased. He was savage when he watched the cliffs and the sea breaking upon them as if they were a face and the sea slapping it. He watched yachts leaning fast their lines and booms lapping and kissing and the water climactically spraying the decks only to rivel away off the wood. This was a good America. This he loved, the America of ships and its deserted sea coast. He thought that Americans did not anymore go down to the sea, nor to their prairies, and he thought this as he watched broken light dimming on the waves. Americans did not go down to the sea, and he saw few of them on the empty moonlike bright beaches in winter when he loved to walk.

He had never questioned an early death. He knew that his life was very strong and intense, that his sadnesses were extremely still and revealing, that the life he had on the Maine coast and off it was good, and that death was no more than leaving the coast.

One summer when the harbor was so full of white yachts they seemed only the plumage of the jetties and wharves, the cutter *Madison* was making its way

out to sea. It was high off the water and unlike the
yachts it traveled with perfect direction. It was on
business and it knew and was the guardian of the waters. It was a father to the little ships and it moved
out to the high seas where they seldom went. Nathaniel was standing on the bridge watching the jetty
pass when he noticed a woman at the end near the
great bell. He stood atop the white wall of his ship
and looked at her, and turned to her direction as he
passed. He saw her whitened face with only touches
of a red glow from the new day, her suede coat with
glittering square gold clasps, her deep violet stock-
ings the artful pattern of which he could see even on
the glaring bridge and which seemed to him the
color of wallpaper in a very elegant house in Philadelphia. He wanted to tell her that, and he did when
he found her two weeks later. She had watched his
ship beaming away from her at three quarter face
out to sea, halyards stretched musically, fittings
aligned as if on compass course. His whole world
fought eastward and rolled from side to side. Military
ships moved fast and appear to rush away. At that
moment they entered into a compact.

The town was small; he found her easily. She was
a lady, she was alone, and she wore a blue and white
dress of lace with tight cylindrical sleeves and blooming cuffs. And her hair was the color of whitened
gold. Whether by time, because of her great beauty,
or by chance, this woman had found just the right
way to dress. They walked down a dirt road between
two fields of white grass and they exchanged information, although it seemed not important. "How old
are you?" she said.

"Twenty, just."

"I am thirty-four, just."

She was married to a lawyer who was going to run for Congress, and she had finished Radcliffe when he, Nathaniel, was eight. But all this was by no means an appraisal or reappraisal, for their minds had been made up the day he saw her as he left for the sea. They talked as if they were engaged in last-minute instructions, hurriedly and without feeling or emphasis, as when stewardesses put on life jackets and pretend to blow them up.

She stopped and looked up at him. Her face was the color of white winter sunshine. It was peaceful, as peaceful or more so than what Nathaniel had learned was the peace of climate and the quiet of a warm day in March when the ponds are thawing and quite glistening. This woman's face was glistening. "I," she said, "should be very upset if I never see you again. If you go away now you will die, whenever you do, and I will die eventually and this meeting, about which I am otherwise very, very upset, will remain suspended here forever for no one ever to know, and I will have let my love spin and not engaged it. If love is the purest thing, and if I love, why then should I not love?"

The answer was not as clear as the imperative, and because they feared that they would never part he found a way. "I must be back at the ship at four. The whistle will blow and it will be heard on every part of the island. I know a barn with apple trees surrounding it. It overlooks the sea and the apples will be good by this time. We can go there, and sit, and do nothing. And when the whistle blows I will look at you, and rise, and run to the ship."

They had apples for lunch and watched the sea. He remembered how she held the apples away from her so the juice would not stain her dress. He remembered how she sat, one leg upon the other. He remembered every detail of this woman, every small feature, every gesture, every move, breath, blink, silence, and sigh. She and her husband were not born in war, and they would live to be old. He would go to Vietnam, and not come back. She smelled fresh and delicious, and when she spoke she paused often and at just the right place to watch his face. He watched her for four hours. He never once touched her. They did not say much, only little things, about the tide, the sun, how hot it was. She was having her youngest day, he his oldest. When they realized they had been simply watching one another for hours they laughed. She had never looked into a man's face for hours. He had never looked into a woman's face at all, at least not in that way. When she had looked into her husband's face, or before that at the faces of men she loved, it had been only momentary. Now she was looking into the eyes of a boy, a stranger, as if they were in another world where men and women lived in dreams and stared themselves into liquefaction.

And a few minutes after four o'clock the steam whistle of the cutter thundered off the sand cliffs and echoed through all the cow meadows and wheatfields of the island. They stood, she sunburnt, lighted, and dizzy, yet calm. Then he left and ran through a field of hay and nettles onto the road.

He was very young when he died but he had been expecting it. He left her in that place, that island on the Maine coast, never to see her again. She grew to be very old. Her life was long, and even when old she was a comely and then a handsome woman. People wondered why, but she would never tell them. She died with the secret with which her younger man had died years before. Early one spring she heard a steam claxon beating like the wings of a bird over the island, and she saw a young man asking her name (she paused to think of the beauty she had been, how full of the sun, how blond, how strong, how womanly and alive) and, as he was leaving and had turned to run down the hill, she called out over the waves battering the shore, in the sun of long ago, Elizabeth Ridinoure.

The Silver Bracelet

The war was not even ended and many more were still to die when she had come over barley and gold plains to Beverley Station Saskatchewan and the English Benevolent Orphanage. She had had a big tag on her with routing instructions, and had been a long-distance Canadian Pacific passenger, traveling from Toronto into country she had not ever heard of or even imagined, since she was Dutch and only five years old. But even as a child she sensed the health and cleanliness of the plains, the pleasant heat, strong winds, and yellow sunshining days. There, was no war. It was untouched, quiet, thick, hot, and growing.

And the wonder had never passed, not in years of looking down a narrow heat-soaked road disappearing into a sea of golden wheat, of a vast windy blue sky with distant crows arched like eyebrows, of emptiness and ocean-like expanse laden with the richest, most intense summer colors. It was to her quite a miracle, a child of the waves come to land, the turmoil turned to quiet, chaos become the agitation of bees above the wheat. A childhood of cellars, attics, and sewers was thrust into the open height of the universe. This great difference, coming unknowing suddenly from the gray to blue and gold, had made her silent and grateful, had stunned her.

Since she had only confused memories of her life, with strong currents of vividness—of her parents, of when her father went out and did not return but was hunted down like an animal away from its burrow—she felt almost as if she had passed into another dimension, or had been moved in time. Even her clothes, because they were so torn and foul, had been taken away by the liberating troops. But they were of cloth her mother had sewed, and when a kindly foreign giant innocently threw them out after putting her into a brand-new pinafore, she felt again the way it was when her parents became lost to her.

Her father had been a jeweler, and from some silver cutlery he found in the warehouse, he made her a bracelet. "Anneka," he said, "this you put on your arm, up here," sliding it up her little arm, "and as you get bigger you put it down more and more until it comes to your wrist. And then you will know you are going to be a woman and are grown up, because you will not get bigger anymore. I know this from many years of making bracelets for little girls." He smiled, expecting that as in days before she would be happy—but children know, and she looked at him with a killing silence which in other circumstances would have been thickness but which was for then a too, too fine intelligence.

The English Benevolent Orphanage was a square of brick buildings around a courtyard. Each building had metal-covered roofs, lead-silver colored with white from the weather. In places the roofs came almost to the ground because the complex was built up against a little green hill, and Anneka took to the leaden metal as if it were a doll or a blanket. She always returned to it, and if she were missing, then Miss Wesley just went to where the roof met the hill and there was Anneka leaning against the smooth gray. Miss Wesley was unable to know that before coming to Canada the only place Anneka had ever seen sunshine was in the valley of a tin mansard roof on top of the warehouse, but Miss Wesley had understanding for silence and what it can say, since she herself had grown up in the midst of a great silent plain. So after a few weeks of fetching and re-fetching the little green-eyed blond girl from the back of the building, why the child returned always to the same spot suddenly dawned on her, and it showed in her face. When the child saw this she burst into tears, and the two rushed into one another's arms. And holding the little girl, Miss Wesley leaned against the metal, which they both touched with their fingers.

From then on Anneka was able to put things behind her. For as inevitably as the winter wheat, she had to grow. Miss Wesley had become her friend, and was quick to discover her intelligence and energy. Within a year she was speaking English fluently and excellently, and she astonished with her sense of ideas and process. Luckily there was a music instructor, and because of Anneka's quick grasp he provided her with a little cello. "Incredible," he said to the headmistress, "she's incredible. These Jewish children take to stringed instruments so marvelously." But you see it was not so incredible, for her mother had played the viola, and it had been the only music she knew, played quietly and slowly only on evenings when wind, rain, or snow could muffle the sound to outsiders. These became Anneka's favorite times for playing, in the evenings or at night in rain, wind, or snow.

The bracelet had descended to the wrist, and what a lovely wrist it was, of a lovely girl who was tall and thin and had dreams of music. She was very beautiful, the lush alert blondness of The Netherlands thinned and polished by northern winds and snow and ice on the plain. She had two years more of high school, which she was to continue in Toronto. And she had set her heart on the Juilliard School of Music in New York after that. It was spring. The weather had not yet turned and was wet and promising. She was in the music room with the little children, teaching them with tom-toms and triangles, and thick sticks painted red. She was at the piano, her sheepskin jacket thrown over her shoulders. She wore her schoolgirl's uniform, a white blouse and blue and green plaid skirt. Rain was wetting the window panes. Beyond, the snow had melted over most of a field littered with straws and stems. It was just before five o'clock and dinner, the least lonely time of the day, which she knew well from her years there was the best time to get the children interested, and so she banged the piano and sang loudly (somewhat affectedly, in a strangely English accent for Beverley Station), for she loved these children and wanted them to be interested in music—if not as she was, then at least so they could carve a mother or father from the objective world, as was so often done in that place.

When she finished, a girl came in and said that the headmistress had asked to see her. "What for?" said Anneka.

"I have no idea," answered the girl, "but you'd better hurry since you have to do tables tonight." Anneka put her music in the piano bench and went out into the hall. The headmistress was a woman who stood before the assembled children, her hands quivering, to lecture on courage and decency—qualities she believed orphans needed more than others to survive in a world where, she counseled them, events and circumstance were forever tearing men and women apart. Sometimes she spoke on this and other themes for an hour or more, looking out the blue windows at a snow-laden sky, forgetful that little girls were arrayed before her. And sometimes she did things they did not understand, as if something invisible had taken hold of her. She might for example suddenly stand in the dining room and berate the happy eaters about their lack of manners and their "disgustingness." This was like a sudden windstorm which came up from nowhere and then just died down. What a terrible sadness it was, for the older girls, to have to fight her. They knew that she would always be there in the place for which they felt affection only because by some good grace they quickly

grew and left it. Anneka had been accepted at the
school in Toronto, and as she made her way to the
headmistress she felt wary only of her own power.

She entered the office of the headmistress, an elegant room, a study and a parlor at the same time. The
headmistress stared directly at her from behind an
oaken desk. Anneka could see through the leaded
glass window a V of wild geese veering toward the
West and a gray cloud. The headmistress wore black
gloves. Her hands clasped delicately together looked
like a monkey. A fire burned in the fireplace making
the room hot and dry.

"Anneka," she began, "you are one of our best
girls—a good student, an excellent musician. In May
you will be leaving us for Toronto. Have you read the
information about the school which I asked Miss Wesley to give you?"

"Yes, ma'am," answered Anneka.

"Well then, did you come across the dress regula-
tions?"

"Yes."

"And did you see that," and she picked up a piece
of paper and read, "girls shall not wear jewelry of any
kind."

"Yes, ma'am," said Anneka, feeling helpless and
hurt.

"This institution," said the headmistress, "exists for
the benefit of all who enter, and that includes those
who have yet to come. We must comply with the
rules of other institutions with which we have close
relationships. I certainly cannot allow one of our girls
to leave here while perpetrating an infraction of the
rules of a school which has accepted her." She smiled,

and then said, "I am afraid, Anneka, that you must
remove your bracelet. Our reputation rides upon it."

"No," answered the girl, terrified.

"What do you mean 'no'? I have explained, haven't
I, why this is necessary?"

"Yes you have, ma'am."

"Then what is your answer?"

"No," she said, "I can't." She was visibly shaking.

"Well then," said the headmistress, "I will have to
write to the school and withdraw our recommenda-
tion. You give me no choice at all."

The school meant everything to Anneka. Where
else could she go? It was music which made her life
a life of love. She had felt so strong, only to be shown
in an instant that she was indeed very weak. But she
would not cut her bracelet. So many times she had
kissed it, and held it with her left hand as she slept.
So many times she had held it to her breast.

Terribly frightened, the headmistress stood up at
her desk, holding a wire-cutting pliers. "Don't cut
it," said Anneka gently and sadly, as the headmistress
approached, opening and closing the unfamiliar in-
strument. "Don't cut it," she said—passive, broken,
and then full of silent tears. The headmistress put the
bracelet in between the heads of the pliers, and with
a soft clip, it was severed from her wrist. Anneka sat
crying with not a sound, her face red and swollen,
her eyes almost unable to see.

Anneka left the room and went down the hall,
guiding herself by placing her hand against the wall
and feeling the wooden coatpegs. Everyone was having dinner. She went to the music room and sat on
the piano bench staring out the window at night fall-

ing over the fields. It was cold and wet outside, blue-black, like a late November afternoon when hunters go home. She raised her head and looked into the darkness. Her tears were dry, and she was very still, whispering to herself, What have I done to you, my Papa, what have I done?

On "The White Girl" by James Whistler

Without sacrifice the world would be nothing. There are cardinal principles by which we grow, and we blend them together with the energy afforded us and the enthusiasm at our disposal for the result which is our life. These were the thoughts she was thinking while she was thinking. Where do I go from here? It seemed for the first time as if her direction were really important, for this time it was not learning, and not condoned, but truly her own. No one was watching and nothing was expected. It was simply her life, a life started in the era of rebellion and played that way to the full so that even she was embarrassed by its excess. Underneath, though, she knew she would come through, even if she felt lost and lonely, looking for a way to vent the passion she was afraid had vanished.

Her husband was a painter who painted her. In the latest painting she was standing in a white dress by

a white marble fireplace. She could not imagine how
he had managed that perfect and balanced fireplace,
for in the Virginia countryside where they lived they
had nothing like it. Both their families were Wash-
ington families, in government. Both had lived
graceful lives and been trained with thorough sever-
ity in great halls. They were precise. He could pro-
duce a rejoinder which made an adversary feel like
a fox flushed from a hole. He could shame his ene-
mies, and she inspired impossible longing in most
men who saw her, even in the paintings, which were
painted with strength and ferocity. They were sure
the world would take notice. It did not. They worried, for he was a fine painter and engraved his principles into his paintings in great depth.

He painted her in a white dress standing by a marble mantel of his memory; her face was beautiful and
contained, framed by soft red hair and small eyebrows. She was clearly the wife of the painter. Even
had she been only his model and his wife were somewhere else she would have gained the true title, for
with the love he used to paint her he had effectively
married. She was his wife, her every footstep to him
something to love, a true love intent upon concert
so specific and intense that it could be shown only
in a painting of skillful black and defeating white
amidst the red smile of his red-haired wife.

He painted her there with flowers, for flowers
were something he could also paint. Her pleading
was no success and he had allowed her to compete
with flowers. She had looked at them during the
painting. They changed, they died, but she looked
at them throughout. They were flowers from the

fields she was walking through, in the midst of an early summer which as setting for dreams is preserved in stormy winters and seasons of emptiness.

She walked slowly, for she was troubled. She did not know if she should believe in her husband the painter and all the flowing idealisms, all the times when he could not paint, the times when everything she held precious and passionate seemed to vanish. That was part of life, she guessed, and only guessed although she was young and part of life she was young enough not to know it too well.

They had wanted to go to a tropical place, perhaps Tahiti, or South America, or even to a non-tropical place like Japan. And then she was reading and had come across the quotation: "New skies the exile finds but the heart is still the same," and said, "Let's stay in Virginia, for in Virginia as everywhere else we can find fragments of what is good."

Dammit, she thought, winding her way through incredible fields that only a writer would write about, the plague of my generation is the plague of all generations, is that we are searching for essences. She, the woman, the young woman of the painting, was now riding a wide-backed courageous horse in sight of a long row of trees, riding and deciding what she would do. Roads there were through this part of the country, dirt roads of brown like the leather of her boots. My husband the painter, his abandonment and the death in his painting, wild, colorful, risk, risk of a thousand men and the courage of a thousand—or the feminine sight of fields in early summer which I see, she thought, what is it—the horse cleared a stream by jumping—what is it, the torrent or the spread green?

A separation was not impossible. He was not a success, but she understood what he was doing enough to occasionally fill her full of love. They had expected a paradise, being from so rich a time. But he had given her great conflict and the burning which can be likened to a prairie fire in the sun. Was it this she wanted or something else? The irresponsible wild crazy burning or a tight set-in shattered life? The burning she would take, like the crashing of the sea against the shore, no craft to that, no skill, just what was artfully raw.

She crossed another stream and started to gallop home, home to a small house, to a husband who painted in falsetto, an intent madman afflicted with the beauty of color.

She spurred the horse across green plains and luxuriant powerful summer fields, summer fields of summer rain and a gray sky which told her that life was short and everything in the simple stroke of a painter's brush. Her husband was a painter. It was part of her choice. What else, she thought, is there in this sober life that makes us good?

She was committed to this man who traded all for essences and captured everything in color. She spurred her horse, over fields, across woods, in the mockingbird spring of Virginia, Virginia of a new world untried and untested like a young woman in white with garland of young hair. Virginia, to her from then on the symbol of courage, the symbol of bravery, the very center of her soul, the first essence she had ever got, true love for the painter.

Everything was a flat field of green bright in the sun, and she rode fast, devoted, decided. She was for him, all throughout. He painted and she loved him, loved him, loved him, as much as he loved her, for the gentle arching of her eyebrows and her mortality made him a man.

Back Bay Conservatory

Boston is a city of libraries and darkness, winter darkness, when lights shine through a cold mist or the clear air. If the wind has come from New Hampshire it is possible to see every star from every street and in the day the blue of the sky is absolute. But if the wind is off the sea the entire city is dark and close, the sparkling crystals not faraway stars but luminous white ice and snow. You can see the snow fall even in the dark, and though there is complete silence each descending particle has its own sound. Libraries shelter students and give the impression that strong fires burn in adjoining rooms. Of course there are no fires but the impression remains as one takes off coat and scarf. At night the windows of reading rooms are black and astonishingly cold.

Victoria had not been named after the Queen but rather her mother's sister who was not, as Victoria said, drowned on the *Lusitania* but killed as a child

in a great fire which took most of the town and left
the rest in despair. It happened one January night
in Vermont before the First World War, and the father of the first Victoria had gone over the border
into Canada to find laborers to build him a new
house. It made no difference; she had been his hope,
the little girl who when burned to death had been
clothed in flannel the color of flame.

Victoria played the piano and was taught by a man
named Andreyev. He kept his studio in a building devoted to music on Massachusetts Avenue near Symphony Hall, near enough anyway so that when Victoria caught a glimpse of it on her way to the lesson
she thought how she always thought of playing to a
mythical audience of professors and music critics.
There were thousands of music critics. They came
from every publication ever published, even Turkish
technical journals and African joke magazines. And
there were friends, all the friends she had ever
known, especially the ones who had slighted her, the
ones who had somehow gained on her in competition
at remote and remembered times, and the front row
was reserved for those she had loved who were no
longer in her life.

Leaning over the piano, Andreyev looked out his
window and saw a golden dome on a hill of brick
houses, and a white dome on buildings grayer than
Westminster. He knew that Victoria often took a
long tour around the hill before her lesson. A magnif-
icent pianist, she was his best pupil. She did not always practice as much as she might have, and was
not as disciplined as many others, but she had so
much love for what she played that she could not

help but play it well. She knew she was good and her career in the literal sense was fast and musical, forward without hesitation; she enjoyed even the strain.

They always talked while her hands warmed. Sometimes when it was very cold it took fifteen or twenty minutes for the frost to pass so that she was dexterous. He wanted to warm her hands in his hands. He might have done it. She wanted him to, but instead they talked about his silver medals. They were won in his twenties and they impressed her greatly. He thought she knew she was going to win gold medals, but she knew neither that nor that at thirty-five he believed himself to be not good anymore as a pianist, only passable as a teacher, and too old for girls of their early twenties—girls like Victoria, whose diversionary walks around Beacon Hill were so that her face might be red and the cold would cling to her coat and refresh the room.

Ascending the staircase she progressed faster and faster, gliding up like a rising angel to the sound of strings from the many rooms all about her. She felt like heat itself rising and when she entered to find serious Andreyev there came to her a sudden reddening which reminded him of all the Provençal and early Italian poetry he had been forced to read, which in Victoria suddenly seemed quite real.

She walked to the window and looked at the vanishing light, at the gold-rimmed snow on buildings, at the flat white basin of the Charles River—not a river because it does not flow—and her heart danced. The sun glinted off her glasses, and her black hair came near the thick white edge of the lens. She had bad eyes but they were large and brown. Her hair was as black as if she had been Chinese, and her face was long and fine. She knew that when she left her lesson it would be dark and she would ride the green-sided trolley back to Cambridge.

After his five o'clock lesson with Victoria, Andreyev usually walked to his small house in Brookline, a house with white rooms and two pianos, a house where there were never any women. In summer when Boston was hot, and Victoria went back to Vermont to swim in the Baker River's rapids, when he was most lonely, when the city seemed quiet and green as if a dream of the Middle East, in summer he thought of departed students and played better than winter ever heard because there was no one to listen.

Andreyev found that his convictions backed him into corners. At first it had been welcome, since he was sure he would eventually triumph. He was all right until his confidence began to erode, after many meetings with other great pianists who in truth were failures. He was at a time in his life when he could not accept failure and yet did not have success. Enough strength remained in him to keep away the comfort of being only a man, blessed with a trade but completely mortal. He was still bent upon being a great pianist—but so feebly and passively that it became just a thought to have on the trolley as he sped across a landscape of gray rain and wet trees. The less he thought of breaking into public life like a long overdue baby bird cracking its shell, the more he delighted in things he had not noticed in years and years since the beginnings of his ambition, and the less he wanted to be alone. He began to be proud of his fierce black eyes, his height, and his Russian-ness—things which for so many years he had consid-ered only for their effect on concert audiences. He bought himself a suit and new glasses, for the old ones were heavy and contradicted his face. He found that when he abandoned his ambition he regained strength enough to become again ambitious. Mean-while Boston passed him on all sides and above, and he lamented that his students were like clouds going to sea as he remained rooted firmly on the barest place of land. There had been a time when he might have given up his dreams, but he had kept them and it soon was too late ever to release them. He felt the twenty years. He was already old enough to dream of abandoning his dreams. He imagined that his girl students were loved by his boy students and that they danced together. Victoria was the kindest of them all, and unfortunately the most beautiful.

With the sun making her gold glasses shine she turned to him and smiled. Her hands were warm, she said, they could begin. She was to play a piece he had adapted from guitar music by Gianocelli. The timing was difficult but he had arranged it well and she had practiced for many hours the day it snowed. She played while he counted time, coming down doubly hard on the stresses he had indicated in red pencil. They went through it three times. Then she played at smooth pace without him. There were mistakes and she once hesitated. She became as red as when she had come in from the cold. Again, he said. She played with no mistakes.

While doing it once more, simply because she liked it, she told him at intervals in the long rests that

. . . she was going to stay . . . in Boston for the summer . . . she was glad . . . and she planned mainly to practice. She wondered if he too were going to be in Boston and if he would have time to continue the lessons.

He walked to the brown marble mantel where his medals were framed on black felt, silver medals all. She was playing with great speed and energy.

"I am going to be in Boston this summer," he said, turning down the frames one by one, "and although I myself must practice I will have time for you. As you know, or perhaps you don't, I haven't performed in eight or nine years. If the summer goes well I plan to give a concert in the fall."

She stopped playing and turned to look at him. "Keep playing," he said, and she returned to play faster and almost as if in anger. "I know it's difficult to play when someone is talking, but people always talk. Gianocelli is especially beautiful. No one knows him and he wrote little but I think he is among the best." There was a silence. "Most of my students are absent in the summer." He looked at her, at her black dress and gold chain necklace. "If you want you can practice here. The windows are open in the summer and the light is better."

She stopped playing and looked out at the blackness of the night which had descended. She was confused, and although she saw like silver on jeweler's felt a thousand white lights of cars moving on the long bridge from Cambridge, she was frightened and could only say, as if she were older than he, Andreyev, Andreyev, Andreyev. But she did not feel older. She couldn't have.

A Dove of the East

They rode up to the Golan every week on Friday or Saturday, in an old army truck with two rows of hard wooden seats. In summer the heights were cooler than the Bet Shan Valley, which like a white strip of ivory is set into mountains as if they had been wounded, and cartilage exposed. Nothing is hotter than an afternoon by the Jordan, neither chilly nor deep but green and rapid like an African river.

When Israel took the Golan she found it to be dry and wasted, brush fire slopes gold only to God and pilots, so she put cattle there, since anyway she had few elsewhere. The price of meat was high; the grass had gone uneaten. Men had to watch the cattle and tend them otherwise they stumble and cannot get up. They fall in gullies. They become trapped in labyrinthine ravines. Ticks make mockery of them, since they have no hands. They step on mines and must be shot. They lose themselves in reverie and cannot find grass to eat. They easily get lost, and at night they are frightened, like primitive men.

The farmers of Kfar Yanina, a settlement in the Bet Shan Valley, sent a proportion of their number to take care of their steers. There had been economic trouble, crops not coming in with all good speed, a shortage of labor as the young left the settlement for the pains of city life, dry years, and fires set by artillery. In a memorandum entitled *What Is to Be Done?* the secretary suggested allocation of loan capital to build a herd of cattle to roam about the hills in the north, where the mountains had snow.

A herd was created. In the first year it numbered four hundred, in the second, six hundred, and in the fourth, one thousand, at which it stabilized for lack of further resource. The farmers already knew how to make fences and enclosures, and how to deal with the animals and encourage their health and reproduction—since at the settlement cows had been in residence from 1936 onwards, the same family, remarkably content to give all that milk and end up as roasts in the ovens; and that is by no means funny, for if you look into the eyes of a cow you see a gentle being, perplexed and confused, and although they are hardly full of grace and beauty they order pity in a human heart for their very thickness and incapacity.

Being practical, the men of Kfar Yanina did not worry about the fates of their charges but rather tried to nurture them into robust meatiness. In the breeding and feeding they were already expert, but they had to learn how to ride and rope, and this they took up rapidly if only for its romance and publicity in films. There were a few accidents. Once, red-haired Avner crashed his horse head-on with a fat steer, causing minor injuries in order of increasing seriousness to the steer, the horse, and Avner, who rode chuckling in an ambulance to the nearest X-ray machine. But all in all they were good herdsmen, and they developed into a permanent élite group within the settlement. Perhaps in doing so they struck a natural balance, for they became extraordinarily desirable to women, who were irresolute and nervous in their presence. This may have been because they saw the women so rarely. For whatever reason, hot fires were lit when the Golan crew returned suddenly out of the dusk for alternation, hot showers, conversation, movies, and dalliance.

But they left their women after a day or two and rode back in the old truck to a little camp of tents and trailers. It was usually on Friday or Saturday. They rested for the evening, then got up the next morning and began to work.

Each day a scout was sent to trace ahead the paths by which the herd, or parts of it, would move the next morning. In that way the scout and the herd moved out simultaneously, the herd stopping at a place determined the day before, the scout continuing into fresh country. As many steers as they had could not have been moved spontaneously and freely—it was hardly a place for Isadora Duncan—for various reasons. The first was the availability of watering places. Sometimes they were wet, sometimes not, and the scout was obliged to find a wet one within a certain distance. The second was the condition of march. One is always surprised by the agility of cattle and their willingness to confront the steep and narrow, but they are after all not goats and it is not possible to drive them over too difficult a path. The third is pasturage, which must be suitable and green; green, that is, in a Middle Eastern sense, which can be yellow. The fourth is that a herd should be able to find new pastures without too much back-tracking, an act which is a waste and which tends to upset them. The fifth is that the herd and the riders must be fairly well protected from saboteurs. Occasionally a steer will fall, victim of a long and casual rifle shot. In that case the riders must turn their own guns against it, and call immediately for a truck to take it for butchering. Steers have been known to set off anti-vehicular mines, resulting in an awful sight, but there is little danger to the men, whose weight even if combined with that of a horse will not trigger the fuse.

A scout must balance these conditions, weighing and judging, until he reaches an acceptable result. He then rides back to camp, sometimes late at night, for he has his work cut out for him. It is a good job though, because he can be alone and he usually rides all day on the mountains and in the canyons, stopping only for a small lunch, to rest his horse, or for the hell of it to sing and eat chocolate and know he stands alone for as far as he can see and sense.

And for every Jew who did this a terrible joy descended. He was a cowboy, standing with a rifle, a rope, a horse. He was strong, tanned, able to move with lightning speed over long stretches of ground, tough, alert, and dirty. And yet he was incredibly sad and thought perhaps he was wrong to ride rather than reflect. Being in the saddle was a fearsome thing. And no matter how natural it seemed or how rough and arrogant he was he feared deep down that he had succeeded, and fearing his own success he rode harder and was more daring and it seemed that he was extraordinarily capable upon a horse.

A favorite and excellent scout, a hard and trustworthy man, was Leon Orlovsky, a French Jew who had been at Kfar Yanina since the Second World War, who spoke little, and who often did the work of two men. He was one of those people with neither past nor future. About him the young, the middle-aged, and the old never thought very much or hard for he was self-contained, a little irrational, and he absented himself from normal society by means of superior work. Had he only been able to deal with people he might have been elected secretary many times, for he was well educated, and although in his fifties, as handsome and masculine as a man could be, like the rare film star who has aged well, or the fit professional soldier who hasn't a mean look. Yet he did not even speak to women, and appeared shy and confused by them. Many women had fallen in love with him from a distance, but momentarily, for he was clearly not to be sought.

For most people he was just a brusque and silent ex-European, an ill-fitting refugee who had strange habits. In his case it was that he wore a tremendous coat into the dining room (when he was on rotation from the mountains) and filled its pockets with all manner of things—eggs, bread, scallions, salt shakers, tomatoes, and whatever else he could fit in—and then left to eat alone in one of the watch towers or among the date trees.

Whatever his peculiarities, and they were many, the young men, army officers in the reserve with new families, knew that they could trust him. As a scout he was unmatched, for he had not only vigor but wisdom. He had in twenty-five years become senior on the land, a master farmer and horseman, as knowing of the winds, soil, and animals as a man can be—and yet he was from Paris.

This Parisian, who walked no longer among the shimmering autumn trees of the Jardins du Luxembourg but instead in the pale green and sulfurous orange date orchards ripe with heat and sweet decay, packed his canvas saddlebags and laid on his equipment with the thoroughness of a legionnaire. "If a man is to be independent," he was fond of saying, "he must be the master of his kit, and pack lightly but with great care."

His horse, the offspring of a Texas quarterhorse and a pure-bred Arabian, had the strong chest and mathematical curves of a desert animal, along with the somewhat thicker neck and sturdy legs of the American mount. A chestnut mare who would have been at home in Virginia, she carried her rider with great speed and over difficult terrain despite the heat and hills. A locally made saddle, cool for the horse, with a palm-wood pommel and an English halter and bit, could not have weighed more than five pounds altogether on her.

His saddlebags were of white duck and in them he carried a liter vacuum bottle of cool water purely for the pleasure of it since he carried two plastic bottles also a liter apiece in the bags and a similar one on his belt. In a little tin box he always put some wheat biscuits, half-dried beef, dried apricots, peaches, and bananas, chocolate, and a Cuban cigar cut in two. He carried an aluminum cup in which were four tea-bags, a small sack of sugar, and matches. In the other half of the bags he had three long magazines of am-munition for his automatic rifle which was in a leather case on the saddle, a small and powerful Carl Zeiss pocket telescope, his book for the week, some toilet articles, and whatever else might end up there (for instance a newspaper or an interesting-looking rock he had found). A warm leather jacket was rolled inside two cotton wool blankets resting over the top of the bags; on his belt in addition to a canteen he had a Parkerized knife in a leather sheath which held also a pliers-wirecutter, a stainless steel awl, and a pocket whetstone. A white although vaguely cream-colored leather lariat which smelled just like his horse hung near his rifle, where he also often put his shirt. He brought the lariat mainly out of habit but also because he sometimes came upon strays which in a long and frustrating process he eventually led home.

With all this, or rather with only this, he stayed away from his companions for a full day, often two, and sometimes three, depending on what he was supposed to find and how easy things were or how difficult. For him this was a great delight. In solitude he could remember, and hope, and in rapturous mo-ments in the early mornings or late afternoons when the sun did not impose its glaring reality he some-times even dared to plan.

"I'm going up ahead," he said to Yossi, the head of the crew, "about five or ten kilometers. I don't think that at this time of year it will be hard to find water. At least it wasn't last year at this time; the damn thing was overflowing. I'll be back late this afternoon."

Yossi nodded his head and said, "O.K., see you then," and Leon, whose Hebrew was not quite perfect and who spoke in a deep and rather sad voice, mounted his horse and rode away. He had arisen before the others, shaved while they slept, eaten while they were shaving, and left while they were eating, with only a few words to Yossi. He passed by the herd quietly and then rode hard and fast for some distance until, surrounded by silence, beige rocks, and fast-rising heat, he came to a ridge which he climbed and followed, seeking out a decent route suitable for cattle.

After an hour or two he thought he had found a good path and rode on it toward the place where the steers were being driven. He could see far off in the distance a light cloud marking their transit. Had he been new he might have departed from the path to that night's resting place at the point where the two were closest. But he could see that although he and his horse could pass through the ravine in between, the herd couldn't. So he left the path a good mile or two before most people would have and followed a gently rolling hill along its topmost ridge. In order to get to this destination along an easy way he sometimes had to travel in the opposite direction, waiting for the hill to curve around again and send him to where he was going. This reminded him of something he had heard a long time before, in Switzerland. He had taken it as a figurative lesson for his life, and then in the Golan he found himself all the time acting out its literal sense.

"In Switzerland," said a tall bland-looking man whom the children called "Monsieur Yaourt," "one must often go down in order to go up." The lights switched off and a projector beamed a blinding ray at a glass-beaded screen. Leon covered his eyes until he heard the film winding through the sprockets and could smell the warm celluloid; he saw on the screen a black and white meadow, and mountains. He recognized on the wall what he saw each day in colors untranslatable in depth and perfection. He then saw a boy much like himself, about twelve, blond, in leather shorts, walking across a log bridge to the beginning of a trail. Klaus, as "Monsieur Yaourt" called him in his narration, was a Swiss boy about to climb a small non-dangerous mountain. Otherwise, he judiciously added, he never would have gone alone. Klaus knew when to set out, when to return, how to climb, and what to take. Klaus had asked his parents or some other higher authority if he could climb the small non-dangerous mountain alone. They had said yes only because he was a Swiss boy used to living in the country. And children from Paris would have to wait until they were older to climb mountains by themselves, small, dangerous, or otherwise. Klaus held up several completely unidentifiable packages and "Monsieur Yaourt" said, "He has taken with him for the ascension cheese, bread, meat, and fresh fruit." Klaus was pictured going down in order to go up, and later after he had raised a large Swiss flag on a heavy pole waiting for him at the summit, going up in order to get down.

Leon noticed the strange mottled gray of the Swiss flag, a flag he knew to be scarlet red, a color not naturally common in the Alps, a color which in black and white has a peculiar heat and grain. And he stared at it with feigned intensity, but not more than that of the girl next to him who had an equally serious look. Each was sure the other was looking and wanted to appear grim and reflective. He was perfectly content to sit in the pinewood hall listening to the rapid clacka clacka clacka of the projector for as long as any film would run even if it were not a Charlie Chaplin because sitting next to him was a girl also from Paris, from the 16th as was he, a girl he had noticed in the station even in the midst of his fear at being packed away to the cool green Alps, a girl with dark red auburn hair and thin long legs and arms. She was tan and beautiful, and was prone to giggling, and tried to show that she did not care that he existed by doing cruel little things like walking away from him abruptly as he spoke, or making fun of him. But she cried every night and clasped her arms around his imagined presence because she loved him so much, so much that it frightened her, for it was a very deep and serious love for a child. Her name was Ann.

In Austerlitz Station, a Paris June, and lines of children waiting for special trains to take them to Brittany, Germany, and the Alps. Leon had come with his father to await the train. The little boy carried a small bag in which was a carefully packed tin of sand-

wiches, chocolate, a penknife, and a French transla-
tion of Mark Twain's *A Connecticut Yankee in King
Arthur's Court.* He wore schoolboy's shorts, a Bristol
blue shirt, and an enameled pin glowing red and
white with the Swiss flag and the name "Suisse." He
was young enough to half think, half imagine that the
pin and small military bag would set him apart as a
youthful Swiss official returning gravely to the country he knew so well, on a mission vaguely connected
with banking, military affairs, and the prevention of
German rearmament. And so he acted haughty and
serious, silent, and in a way he thought to be adult.
His father, a gentle but tough-looking man who had
seen the Great War almost from its very beginning
to its absolute end as a press officer assigned to all battles on all fronts, accompanied him and stood there
in a gray suit with a Legion of Honor pin he had
earned by filing thousands of dispatches to inform
the public of the carnage. He had started with fine
description, casting a good eye on the rapid clash of
those two armies and the suffering countryside underneath, and had ended half-alive, with reports as
clipped and sad as Morse code. But during the war
he had fathered a son, an only son, who brought him
back alive and restored his humor.

While standing by his boy he passed greetings to
other fathers he knew or with whom he was ac-
quainted, and this included a doctor of considerable
wealth and age who lived in the same district and frequented the same restaurants and bookstores. The
doctor's daughter was tall and looked older than her
age: she had the most beautiful mouth and eyes
Leon's father had ever seen, and when he saw her

as he greeted her father he felt as if he were looking simultaneously into the past and the future. He was understanding what his son could only feel, that the life of their generations was here reborn, and blessed, and compassed; Leon in his confusion had only a sense as strong as memory of all his life, while shattering whistles reverberated between shafts of dusty light as trains ended or began what trains exist for.

They did not reach Kreuzlingen on the Baden-See until the middle of the next day, when the children were exhausted and gray despite the freshness of the air and the hunting-horn atmosphere. They could see Germany on the far side of the lake, and since borders were for him always the most exciting places in the world, clear demarcations promising something different and new throughout their entire lengths, he spent much time that summer watching the high clouds crossing to Germany with the grace of gliding dirigibles. And the light from them was so much more superb, separating into currents, corridors, and rays of gray and silver. The frontier was then a place of prosperous romance, the fields of Bavaria enameled green and settled nightly with cold clear mist were as joyous and beautiful as a twelve-year-old boy could have wished. He was a Jew from Paris and beginning to open up on the world, with these his first views royal—something he considered later, achingly, a mean trick of a God whose savage beauty made sharp mountains of ice and rock rise suddenly out of soft green fields.

When he came finally upon the place he had found several days before and to which he had guided one of the men (who was then in the process of guiding the herd), he dismounted to rest and water his horse. He removed the bridle and bit, unfastened the rifle scabbard and saddlebags, hobbled the horse, and let her drink.

In the same way that he had years before rationed out his lunch on the way to Kreuzlingen so that different sandwiches were assigned to various cities and the chocolate was divided between Lausanne and Zurich, he had determined that upon reaching the watering place he would have four squares of chocolate, one biscuit, a dried apricot and banana, five sips of water from his belt canteen and one cup of cold water (because it was the middle of the day and as hot as new steel). He ate slowly and with great pleasure—one thing after another, orderly, disciplined, and lasting. He was the same with his meals, which he planned, and with his room, which was as neat as his kit. This was because there was something of a German in him: he loved ordered beauty and success in objective things. When a young man he had learned German to study science. And he looked English, so that he was often mistaken for a Briton or a German, this giving him great satisfaction for it has always been popular in one way or another to be a master of the world or even just to resemble the type. But more important than that, he simply was an orderly, organized man and always had been. Many people disliked that or saw it as a sickness, but he could not see why, and anything under his control became almost immediately as shipshape as the bridge of an English cruiser. This was good for running things, judging disputes, understanding the way things worked. He was a good scout because he ordered the shape of the land in his mind and made calculations as to where and when to go. People who simply threw themselves at the land and did not weigh and judge its characteristics usually fell in the ravines or ended up red-faced on the army road. "In that case," said Leon, "it would have been just as wise to have sent a cow."

After about half an hour he packed up and rode out, backtracking along the winding ridge to the path he had found earlier, arriving after several hours on a wide plateau with soft earth and a few palms scattered here and there. He was riding in a little grove of trees, trying to find open water or a well, when he noticed that it was getting late. Perhaps, he thought, I will sleep here for a few hours and then go back when the moon has risen. It's clean here, and the leaves make a nice sound in the wind. In fact he was very happy about camping in the grove because it seemed somehow European. It was several acres of small trees, some palms, and many pines, and quite a few deciduous saplings whose leaves were like bronze medallions. Then he began galloping his horse through the brush, to beat it down, to find water, to find the best place to sleep, and just for the sake of galloping itself.

He was an excellent horseman, having studied for eight years at a Viennese riding academy in Paris, and although the trails past Versailles were not as rocky and hilly as those on the Golan he had absolute confidence. When he had arrived at Kfar Yanina—a half-bearded, ragged Frenchman spit from the hold of an illegal immigrant ship—the man who tended the few horses told him, fearing an accident, to keep off. He had done it with such contempt and superiority that Leon grabbed one of the saddled horses from him, mounted it suddenly, and began to go as far as he was able through his graduation exercises. Needless to say, the saber charges, jumps, mountings and dismountings while on the run, and highly controlled form were the beginnings of his reputation at Kfar Yanina.

And there in the grove he drew his lariat as if it were a saber, this perhaps the most exciting instant in the life of horse or horseman, waited the tense moment, and then charged with great speed—cavalry, another fine and useless art he had inherited from the past, part of his world which had vanished. He was like cavalry, speeding by trees and charging down another row with the quick turn only a quarterhorse can make; both horse and rider became heated and their blood ran fast. It was good to be sometimes like a Mongol, a Scythian, any hard fighter who used everything to find strength where there was no strength, courage where there was no courage, swirling cold air to beat against the fire of his activity. He shot down the rows breaking the grasses, the horse's hoofbeats echoing callously through the trees. He took his rope and with it beat at the trunks of the palms, strapping them fiercely as if they were an enemy. And then he paused at one end of the grove, red and wet, his blood surging through him, his lower jaw trembling, and he began to scream at the trees. He said no words but his voice, like that of an attacking animal, could be heard at a great distance—even though no man was there to hear. The horse was frightened and her eyes went round and back. The wind stopped, and almost as if he had been trying to drown its rustling through the branches above him Leon stopped too and tears began to fall from his eyes all over the saddle and his horse's wet back. He cried for a long time, and then dismounted and slept.

When he awoke, it was dark. He could see by the light of the stars his horse standing a few feet away, looking at him as if to say, If you do this again, I'll go. He stood up and tended the horse, reassuring her, and then, feeling as tired and drained as he could, he began to make his own little camp. He broke some branches to build a fire for tea, which he drank while he ate some biscuits and beef. Usually when he made camp it was a tight as a drum, but this time everything was scattered. He was just too tired to impose a design on the few things he had lying about him. He spread his blankets, jammed a magazine of ammunition into his rifle, and lay down to listen for an hour or so to enter the frame of mind which would assure him alertness to any strange sound, even while he slept. Rifle by his side, he started the silence.

In between shudderings of the trees he heard a whistling, a weak deathlike wheeze at regular intervals off on his left. He waited, not knowing what it was. It sounded like a child's idea of a witch's sigh, a frightening noise from and within the darkness. It was, and this he sensed for sure, a steady death rattle. He waited more, and his lethargy fled from him as fast as alcohol disappears on the ground. Now he was

planning and alert; like a bat he turned his head to
and fro, searching the coordinates of the sigh to see
if it were moving, while all the time checking the opposite silent sides where he expected surprise. No
grasses rustled except in the wind, but perhaps it
moved only then? It didn't, because it stayed in the
same quarter.

If it were an enemy, what would be the sense in
alerting him—perhaps to frighten him and steal his
wits away, perhaps to confuse? But the man who
could make such a noise was beyond Leon's imagination or experience. So terrible and pathetic was it
that he thought perhaps he was mad. Remembering
how he had screamed at the trees and beat them, he
feared that they were whining in the darkness, and
bleeding, and wailing like broken bodies. His fear
grew white in front of him.

Then in a half beat of his heart he became less
afraid and instead angry; he could see the darkness
again, and the stars. He pulled his boots all the way
on, and determined but fearful started toward the
sound ever so quietly, rifle in hand with its safety off
and his finger on the trigger, ready to fight without
fear when the moment came, as he had done several
times before in war. Yet he knew that he had to judge
finely, for it could be an innocent making that hideous noise. He, of all men, was alert to that. And perhaps because of that he did not fire when he ranged
in on it and fixed its exact location, but kept walking
toward it, transfixed by its steadiness and by its weakness, as if the faint whistle were air rushing past the
fine points of the stars. It was closer than he thought

and without intending to he came directly upon it. He saw what it was.

"Oh God in heaven," he said. It was a dove. He had trampled it with his horse and it was dying.

Having only the light of the stars, he could see no colors. But he had lived in the same shade as doves for a quarter of a century, and was able to deduce from patterns and shadings in the black and white the colors he knew so well—a process which signified for him the depth of his life. It was an Eastern dove, not a shock of white and pure line as in the West, but many-colored, as deep contradictions ran through, and it was beautiful.

The wings of a dove are white-tipped, slate gray, brown as the Nile, then bronze along the back to a gold rim at the neck. A turn of the head changes the colors. The neck feathers have a shimmering purplish tinge. Similarly, the slate gray tends to green or blue. Watching it fly is like watching a storm on a tropical sea; the rich hot colors well up and spread across its surface like rain on blue green. Its head, as smooth as a hawk's silken hood, or an airman's leather helmet, with large brown eyes, is patterned with circlets and triangles and rims of white—like a Persian woman made up. It is always tending itself, and flies gracefully amid the olive trees and to date palms, winging and gliding in the clear air of the white hot valley.

But this dove was sick and silent, except for its sigh which had stopped when Leon came upon it, as if it had expected to die. Its wing lay extended, clearly it had been broken, and at the point where wing and body fused Leon could see a deep unnatural depression. Its head was tilted to one side somewhat strangely, and its eyes hàlf closed in pain and waiting. It lay on a fallen palm branch, legs wedged between the thin green leaves.

He simply could not leave it there in its labored breathing to die in the cold and dark, with no one, no other dove, to form a chain from eye to eye, to show love at the last moment, to be there until one was not needed. To die alone is to die a perpetual death, forever unfinished like a straight course into the black of the sky. To die alone is not to have lived. So he took his knife and clipped the palm branch to form a tray, pruning off the extremities and the weak pointed tips of the leaves, and he carried the dove back through the underbrush to his camp. There he rekindled the fire and put the dove and its tray on a folded blanket. He could see in the firelight all the colors he had assumed, and the white ringlets. The dove stopped sighing, and with renewed energy managed to open its eyes a little and turn its head to watch the fire, and Leon, and the white nettles and grasses which were shining in the light of the flames.

For a long time he just stared at it. He tried to give it cool water but it would not drink. He tried to give it fruit he diced with his knife, but it would not eat. Then he laid aside the fruit and water, and after putting more twigs and some heavy branches on the fire, lay down propped on his elbow near the dove, and stared at it trying to decide what to do.

He could not heal it; that was impossible. He could, however, wait with it until it died or until it got bet-

ter. The chances that it would live were greater that
way, since he thought it would eventually take food
from him and thus not starve. But it might take days,
he thought to himself, and meanwhile Yossi and the
herd are waiting for me. If I don't come it will be bad
for all the animals, each one of them a thousand times
this light dove, and dozens of men will be sent to look
for me. And they probably would not find me. When
I returned, what would I tell them? And if they did
find me, what would I tell them then? They would
think me crazy and never trust me again, but how
can I leave this dove?

Leaving the dove was out of the question. When
he looked at it he knew he would have to wait with
it, despite ugly things that would be said, and stories
that would go around. Life was not rich there, and
people depended on the welfare of the animals.
Were they to know why he stayed away from the
herd for days and days, jeopardizing its course and
making everyone worry, they would never forgive
him. And where would he go? And what profession
would he follow?

They would say, Why so much trouble just for a
dove? Do you not eat meat, and chicken? And since
he did, he would not be able to answer them. They
would say, You were irresponsible in your job, and
you paid no attention to the welfare of several hundred men, women, and children. For what? For a
dove that was going to die in any case? And he would
not know what to say to them. But he could not leave
the dove, and as the night passed he lay by it as if
it were a sick child, tired himself, half dreaming. He

lay there as if in a fever, breathing as slowly as the dove, determined to see it through.

Passing a gun shop in the Champ de Mars one fall he felt a great longing to be quail shooting. But he had not had, and had never had, nor would he ever have the slightest desire actually to shoot the quail. He wanted to be dressed in strong leather boots, in khaki pants with pockets on the thighs, to wear a rust-colored tweed jacket with shooting patches, a bandolier of copper bullets, and to carry a deep black shotgun of fine craftsmanship and light weight. He wanted to make his way across country (there was a specific image of gold and yellow grass and a view of low hills and apple orchards) and to come out of the darkness finally with cheeks reddened from the cold and an alert demeanor, to a fire and hot tea. But he had no desire whatever to shoot them. Hunting was merely a slaughterhouse with country accouterments. Why not simply abstract and abandon the slaughterhouse? And yet he ate meat, and would continue, for cruel inconsistency was part of what made life. He became sick when he tried vegetarianism. A proselytizing friend of his who suggested it was thin and the color of ashes in the fireplace flue. Those who saw him, immediately thought of the morgue; there was just something smooth and dull about his gray face—a lack of stolen energy and the evil sparkle of the predator. But for sport? Never, it was just the equipment, the sounds of walking through dry clean brush, the ice cold small rivers by which to halt.

And he loved so much to love that he wondered if he were drawn to it by all but love itself. Walking in the Champ de Mars, a place of orange and blue awnings and quiet curving streets, he felt at twenty so hypnotized by love, by its idea, by the beauty of the women he saw. He stared at them—not with the pompous, self-worshipping, suspiciously homosexual gaze of the Mediterranean strutter, but rather with an openness and humility, a simplicity which for a numbing moment worked its way even to his fingers and back and caused the whirling of an electrified moment to become a feeling of history. History, the means by which he loved, the recollection of all men and all women gazing at one another in times past; the graveyards of Paris, strangely untended and quiet as before a war, full of charted lives which had seen such hot permanent moments as he felt on the Champ de Mars, the hollowness and waste of societies of men and their deeds in the face of these breathless confrontations when the world went silk and eyes moved as if they could feel.

And how refreshing it was afterwards to go back and reflect once again on things and quantities, the books in his shelves, the small everyday machines, speculation, conversation, a new suit of clothes, buttered bread and tea in a café on mornings before school, the grandeur of what he studied, and the excitement of a winter night at work under his light inscribing equations in fine pen across the pages of a blank book.

But these were only the general, and Ann the specific. He had fallen in love with her in the station years before, and then again at the camp when she had spurned him, if only because she loved him too much. With Ann it was not a question of silken moments, but just Ann, not a single association, just Ann. Her singing at Kreuzlingen had so much entrapped him in a lifelong love that he remembered each day several times the way she was sitting at night by the fire, in a blue jacket, her dark auburn hair falling beyond her shoulders. Her voice was clear and especially beautiful, and she was embarrassed to sing, but she sang and her French songs rang out among the hills. For him they still sounded there, having survived all the years of ice and snow, the new roads and buildings, the children getting older and dying. Her songs were still heard.

Later in Paris he knew her at school, loving everything she did. But for several years it was just dreaming, for they hardly even spoke and their manner was such that anyone else never would have had the vaguest notion that they were aware of one another, much less passionately in love. And then one day she broke her ankle on the playing field and he carried her up the steps to his car and drove her to the hospital. He had never touched her except accidentally or to take something from her hand. When he held her, her arms around his neck, he sensed for the first time that far from hating him she loved him; that she thought of him just as he had thought of her, in enveloping dreams; that she was thrilled by his presence as much as he had always been by hers; that she wanted to kiss him; that he was loved back. Then there was a golden fall when he scouted for perfect places in the woods and took her there on weekends. Her hair, lightened in the summer, fell from her blue student's cap. The weather was dry and cool and wavelike winds moved the trees and grass like breathing as they lay together for the first time in the diminishing October sun, its rays weakening into a cool sigh.

His aspirations were as great as his experience was little, but he could do no more than enjoy the impressions he felt so keenly. Life was a powerful confusion with rewards to those who did not control it. Those times were marked by the strangest remembrances: the heavy wooden door of her house, the black metal of his car, the letters they wrote, how Spain had passed them by and they had been hated for being so finely able to achieve what all the world's revolutions and all the red armies, what neither fascists nor pilots nor propagandists, nor the righteous or the daring or the obsessed, could do—and that was to create a heaven on earth. They had been hated for not noticing the definitive and terrible approach of the whitest winter ever to be seen. But had they feared and been oppressed by just the pressure of its advance, then they would have had nothing at all.

In no time they had finished university and found themselves hurtling through the June fields of Normandy on a fast black train, one car of which was filled with their families and friends on the way to the wedding at Honfleurs. He was uncomfortable at the wedding itself: they thought it too beautiful and too much a part of the nineteenth century to be their own, but they wanted the old men and women—for whom the white dresses and morning suits, the flowers and childrens' carts, the canopy, glass, and ring, were real—to be happy and to remember, as memory was all they had. But the great thing for Leon and

Ann was the train ride itself, something which had
not been planned as enjoyment.

They all met at the North Station early in the
morning when the streets were still wet and being
swept. A cool wind came into the train shed from the
north, and everyone was dressed informally but
Leon, who wore a three-piece black suit with two
fountain pens in the vest pocket. He had just published a paper in an important journal of biochemis-
try and won recognition as the *Majeur* of his depart-
ment. This was published with his picture in all the
newspapers of Paris and people had been recogniz-
ing him on the street—not many people, but some.
The car they had reserved was supplied in each compartment with champagne, fruit, and cheese. Leon
and Ann went from one group to another, being
toasted in each compartment and drinking back
until they became riotously intoxicated and staggered down the corridor as the train lurched back
and forth, sending them crashing into walls and
doors. In one place they played cards for half an hour
with an old uncle of hers, in another they received
gifts—for her a black gem of some sort set in a gold
foil, for him more fountain pens, the kind with an
edelweiss on both ends which looks just like a Star
of David. All the time unbeknownst to them they
passed the rusted cannon and common graves of the
Great War. The old men and not so old men looked
out the windows at places they had heard of or
fought in, never dreaming that they would have the
opportunity to glide by so peacefully in a car laden
with champagne. They thought quietly and looked

at the new summer fields; some of them managed to smile.

After the wedding they stayed at Honfleurs boating and swimming. When they returned to Paris, it was the middle of summer and they settled down to work. She often wore a white silk dress and a white hat. They went to museums and walked in the parks at night—it was almost as if Paris were again the city of the century before. But winter came, and then the next summer, and the twentieth century clicked suddenly back into place like the sharp closing of a rifle bolt. Again they were on a train, he and Ann, with just the beginnings of real fear about what Paris would become. Early one morning his father had driven to their apartment and burst in during breakfast looking like someone they hardly knew. "You must get out of Paris now, immediately," he screamed. His son's reaction was one almost of dumbfoundedness; he began to compose himself for analysis of the risks and probabilities, but the father took him by his dressing gown and lifted him from the chair. "Listen to me. I tell you to leave and go south. It is not at all like the last time, for Paris is going to burn, and we will burn first of all. You must leave."

"But how can we, Papa? You are here, and Mother, and Ann's parents and the family. The banks are closed, what nonsense, I am not even dressed," he said somewhat sheepishly before he was slapped across the face and knocked down. He then began to understand his father's understanding.

"All right," he said with a red eye, "we will leave." They dressed, he took his bank books and magazine article, and the three of them drove to the house of

Ann's father, who agreed to leave that day because he too felt it was the opportunity, and "If they don't take Jews as I suspect they will, then we can return. We will always be able to say, if anyone should think to ask, that we are on holiday." He thought because he was so old that he should take charge.

"Monsieur Orlovsky, take the children to the station. We will follow later today after I arrange some business. If all goes well, shall we meet in Aix at the house of Pellegrin?"

"Good idea," said Leon's father, a bit of the fight returning to him, "we will all go separately and meet at the Pellegrins. The children this morning, we in the afternoon as there is some business that I too must finish before leaving, and you at night."

He took them to the station and gave them money enough for several weeks' travel. "I want to see Mother," said Leon, and his father replied that he would see her at Aix and shortly. And then as it became clear that the train was going to leave, the father kissed Ann as he would have kissed a little girl, and turned to his son.

"Until Aix," he said, but just stood there with his hands at his sides. "At the house of Pellegrin." A column of soldiers marched into the back of the station filling it with the rough cloth color of their uniforms. The father, who had seen and lost so much, embraced his son and they gripped one another as if for the last time. Leon remembered his father's tweed jacket, and the smell of cigars even on the shoulder. He remembered how suddenly his father looked so old, and how the old man had grasped his hand with a pathetic strength as if to say, Although we could never communicate and cannot communicate now, I love you very much. And then he backed away and said, lifting his head a little, "Your wife." Leon nodded, climbed on the train with Ann and turned to see his father for the last time standing in a Paris station looking hopeful and childlike, in a black and white tweed jacket which was easy to see against the soldiers' cloaks of the darkest gray. The train pulled away, and Leon feared for him. When they had embraced he noticed how the power of his father's grasp had so lessened with the years. And he thought of the tweed jacket pushing its way through the masses of soldiers.

This train fell southwards instead of climbing north. The fields and trees were crazily indifferent to streams of refugees along the roads. It seemed to Leon that this was yet another battle in the Great War, for much of the equipment looked the same and the feeling was that the dead had risen to take revenge upon the living, that the trenches had suddenly burst open from the pressure of all that had grown within, and that a hideous rotted whiteness was about to envelop the land.

Unlike their wedding train, this one was not rapid. It often pulled over onto sidings for several hours, sometimes for the night, and it had a curious habit of going backwards for scores of kilometers and then coming to a dead halt in the middle of countryside as quiet and lush and black with night as in a dream. Then the conductors would walk up and down with red lanterns, the current would cease, and a tiny old man's voice weave its way through the corridors saying, "Stop for the night. Sleep outside or in. Leave at daybreak."

The trainmen replied to all questions with upraised shoulders and eyebrows. "It is war," they would say, "not a café."

"All the trains have been requisitioned," said Ann authoritatively, "and therefore our parents must have gone in a car. This must be. They are already in Provence." Leon kept busy buying food, bribing conductors to return to him his seat, and looking over and over again at his article as if it might have given him answers. On one of the seats a soldier had left a pea-green great coat with many pockets. With the practice of an established refugee Leon appropriated it, and used the pockets on food-gathering expeditions. He even brought back a bottle of good perfume for Ann, who was as overjoyed as if she had been impoverished all her life. He remained clean-shaven because a barber was also fleeing Paris and had brought his artillery. When the train halted the barber cut down oak branches and heated fresh river water in a large vat he had paid a soldier to steal, and then shaved most of the men on the train in return for food or money, and sometimes for free, just because he missed his home and his shop and the streets he knew so well.

Several days passed, and although Leon and Ann had been used to leaving Paris in the morning and arriving at Aix that evening they were still somewhere in the middle of France—surrounded by cursing farmers, refugees, and confused army detachments hurrying in retreat as if to a battle already won. The life itself was not so bad, somehow there was always fresh food, the weather was good, but his impatience was tremendous regarding the house of Pellegrin, good friends in Provence sure to help. He was sure that his parents, even if they had started by train, would have then taken a car and gotten to Aix after a pleasant journey through the countryside in new summer. Undoubtedly they were in Pellegrin's garden, reading and talking. "My country is being invaded, and yet she contrives to be beautiful." It was early then for Provence, perhaps a little quiet, but a summer bursting out amid the mountains and white-faced cliffs. "I am sure they are there, and they must wonder about us. It is war after all and the sirens are real enough."

Ann, on the other hand, did not seem to worry, but was instead very quiet and happy. This angered him but he said nothing, thinking her very selfish for her lack of concern: she behaved like a schoolgirl on an outing, a little crazy, and he thought that callous indeed, but it only made him love her more.

There was a halt again after yet a few more days, in a small town which they guessed to be in the Midi (it was difficult to tell after being shuffled around for days on nameless sidings and rusted one-track lines). The engine hissed down, the electricity ceased, and the voice of the little old man passed through the train, "Leave tomorrow morning, express South, all tracks now clear, no hotels here." In an instant the passengers had their cooking tools and orange crates alongside the train turning the freight yard full of military trains and matériel into a temporary camp. But this was not unusual as all of France had become a camp of one sort or another.

Leon threw on the coat and checked his wallet. "I will get some food," he said, "before it's all gone."

"Please, try to get some meat or fish."

"Maybe there will be a restaurant. Then I will return with just an invitation—steak, watercress, and wine."

"Of course. I'll dress for the occasion in my dress. Go before it's too late."

He jumped from the train and ran enthusiastically over the many tracks and through the munitions until he came to the town, where restaurants were closed, except for one just for soldiers. There were some farmers with old trucks, selling vegetables and poultry. He bargained with them and afterwards stuffed a chicken, leeks, and potatoes in his big pockets. The coat was unbearably hot but the pockets served well. Again it would be chicken soup, not bad, but he wished he had some beef, especially since Ann had asked for it. Because it was hot he walked slowly back to the yards singing to himself a Jewish song he had learned in camp: "The Day Will Come." Off to his right he heard a humming noise like swarming bees but with a sharpness which offended the ear. Over the glowing terra-cotta tiles of an old house he saw six dots coming almost directly for him from a sky of very pleasing blue. They came so fast that he hardly knew what was happening until they began in terrifying immediacy to strafe and bomb.

At first he had no idea of the target, but then his sense of general danger became a much greater fear. Obviously, they were after the train yard. He began to run, his heart giving him much energy by its beating and fear. It was only after he saw the fighters diving at the yards that he decided to throw off his heavy coat with all the food, and even then he paused for half a second to take his wallet, without which he knew he could not survive.

Bombs were exploding all over the yard, tracer bullets, barely visible in the sun, making puffs and ricochets on the earth and steel. It was the part of a bombing attack comparable to starting a cold engine. Inside, things had not begun to catch, and bombs often fell isolated and without effect. But there were six planes and it was not long until the engine began to go—secondary explosions, walls of flame, freight cars blown apart so that their sides and doors flew like chaff.

He was running as fast as he could, with the incredible grace and energy of instinct. He never in his life had run so fast, nor had he been as sure of foot or as quick to dodge as then in the freight yard.

The train on which he had spent the previous few days was pulling away. The engine had gotten up steam, a track had opened, and it was gathering speed. Ann was in the window of their compartment, throwing things out the window and herself about to jump. "Leave them," he shouted, "stay," even though he was far away and the train was really beginning to move. He cut over toward it with incredible speed. He could hear feet that seemed not to be his own pounding the earth and stones. All was well; he had gone between the fires and bombs and shells, and he was running magnificently. "Stay," he screamed to Ann even as she pulled away with the train, because he knew he would make it. He tried to open one of the doors, but it was shut tight. He began to panic, for he knew there wasn't time for her to help him and the train was passing over cross switches on which he lost a lot of speed.

But then she said, "Other side, other side," and he felt great relief remembering that there the doors were open. He stopped for breath, nodded his head to her confidently, and pointed to the other side of the train. He would wait, get some wind, and then when the back of the train had passed him, make a break for the open doors. She understood this and they were confident that he would succeed. He stood there while the accelerating train passed him car by car and the bombs fell all around. But not one had struck the train, and he had not been wounded at all.

When the last car passed he set out with everything he had, leaping across the rails in one jump, and running furiously to an open door which was banging to and fro. He had room and time to spare. Even though the train was already going fairly fast he could have run beside it and entered by any door, but he wanted to be safe and he began to close on the first. He knew he could do it. It had become a great adventure—what a story to tell. He was sorry about the coat and the food, but he still had his wallet. He and Ann would be safe; he smiled.

And then he heard a terrific roar. A fighter plane's engines came so close he thought it was going to hit him. The deafening noise was followed by a string of explosions rapidly overtaking him. They were incendiary bombs, phosphorus. One exploded some meters in front of him and the world went white. He could see nothing, and he tripped and flew forward crashing onto the railbed of stones and slate. He heard whistles, bombs, and engines, and then lost consciousness thinking he was dead.

When he opened his eyes it was pitch dark except for some orange fires far away. He could hardly see, but that was nothing. Ann was gone.

The old conductor had said the South of France. He raised himself and tried to sense what was around him, thinking only of how to get to the house of Pellegrin in Aix where she and his parents would be waiting.

With much difficulty he stumbled across the rails until he heard a train passing slowly in front of him. He judged it a freight and somehow managed to catch hold of a ladder on its side and climb to a hatch through which he let himself fall without much caution. He landed on bales of some sort of cloth, perhaps felt or even velvet, and lay on them quite comfortably except for his wounds and some burns on his feet and ankles. He could see the sky through the opening, but not the stars, as he was partially blinded. The train had been a shadow, but since they had lived in the summer near the railroad he was always able to distinguish different trains even without sight of them.

Passenger trains were light shells, whisked effortlessly after the engine in delightful relief. The slower freight trains continued to grind the track as had done the engine, with little contrast. Once in a great while he had seen flat-bed trains loaded with tanks and half-tracks. Always on these one could see soldiers perched on the vehicles. Regardless of the time or place they seemed to have the same expression, a combination of the joy of riding carefree and a grim feeling of predetermined death. They would be either eating, casting off nut shells or fruit pies into the wake of their convoy, or scanning the countryside while at the ready on double-barreled machine guns in flimsy sand-bagged positions. It was like riding the back of a dragon. Before the war he had echoed Ann's feelings, that there were too many tanks and soldiers and that these were likely in themselves to bring about conflict, like the spontaneous generation of snakes from a horse's hair in rainwater. But lying on bales of cloth which had been packed before the war and would be unpacked during the war, he wished there had been more tanks and guns, since a lack of them hadn't stopped anything. And he wondered why Ann, who was so weak and willing to be weak, had been attacked as if she were armed to the teeth. With this thought, and a terrible hollowness and fear that at last he had been broken, and in one blow, he fell asleep on his bales under stars he could not see on a train which by pure luck was quickly making its way south.

He was startled suddenly upon waking up in a motionless silence. A blue sky shone through the hatch, and for the first time in days he was able to see perfectly. He had been lying on bales of black felt. Several bees had flown into the car and were having difficulty finding their ways out. The air was different so that he knew he was far away from the yard and sidings of the bombing attack. He looked at himself and felt his face. The cuffs of his pants were burned away and his ankles blistered. His clothes were ripped and full of dried blood, and he felt a wound on his skull and across his forehead. Really awakening he breathed in tensely and thought of Ann. He felt his wallet in his pocket, cursed himself, and prayed that her train had gone directly south. He climbed out of the dark into a freight yard in Provence, in a town he knew well. For some reason, even though he had money, he set out by foot for Aix, fifty kilometers distant. But he was more exhausted than he thought and when he stopped to rest by a bridge he fell asleep and did not awaken until evening. Then he drank water from a cool stream and his rest, the fresh water, and the descent of evening made him feel again like a man. Nevertheless he did not look like one, and when he stopped a truck loaded with mirrors for a ride to Aix the driver would take him only if he rode in the back. "You are ugly, that's why," the man said, and Leon watched himself for an hour or more in the very dimly lighted mirrors. He looked like a Napoleonic infantryman in the Russian winter. This, the fact that he had survived, and the joy at closing the distance between himself and his wife whom he imagined in the garden at the house of Pellegrin made him laugh out loud over and over. He was rugged. What a tale to tell the Pellegrins. He was alive and soon he would see Ann. But his wounds began to pain him and he realized how hungry he was.

The driver rapped on the panel of his compartment. "Aix, Aix," he said, and Leon climbed out just before the truck drove off into the dark. He was in the main square by the fountain and could not believe what he saw.

Literally scores of young men and women, in tuxedos and white ball gowns, were clustered around the fountain, talking and laughing, with champagne glasses in their hands. Telling the virtues of the town, the fountain splashed clear water on clear light. The night was one of those early summer nights which is thick and beautiful and yet cool enough to accommodate the pale light of the moon. They had just graduated. To him it was unbelievable.

He went to the fountain and washed himself. Several of the young people came up to him and one boy handed him a glass of champagne, saying, "Don't drink from the fountain, drink this." Leon drank it with the speed of a trout catching a fly, and he was poured another, and then several others until his pain was gone and he began to feel some energy and a great deal of dizziness. They had gathered around and were looking at him as if he were a nice little dog. He felt no anger, and just looked at them and at the lights and water. "I was one of you," he said, "indeed I was, and in just a few days I have become someone else, never to return. Consider that. Consider that here in your summer of trees and fountain." He was swaying back and forth, not unpleasantly, and his eyes could not focus.

"There is an ice age up there you know, in the North. It's falling down here and will slide over here any time. You know that. You know what's happening." The boy closest to him nodded. He had finally spoiled their party, a spoiled party anyway. Here was a wretched creature who said he was from the North, and they became frightened down to the soles of their patent leather shoes. "There's a war, a war, and I was in it," he said. He began to weep, swaying back and forth, staring into the fountain and its intoxicating random envelopments, stunning the adolescents all around him. "Take me to the house of Pellegrin," he commanded forcefully. Two boys helped him to their car.

The effects of champagne retreated as the little car weaved its way, headlamps beaming, through the walled and gardened countryside quiet but for a din of crickets and the rushing of dark overhead branches. They left him at the gate and he walked up a familiar stone drive to a familiar house which was shut, and dark, and terrifying; and he wailed a cry of despair and horror which silenced the night animals, for even they could sense the upwelling of Hell.

In September of 1947, after he had been with the Free French, and then for several years searched as best he could the D.P. camps and the German records, he went to Palestine. Both sets of parents had never left Paris except on a train to Poland. Beyond names and numbers there was nothing more to be heard of them. They had vanished into the soil. They had not even a grave. He returned to the family houses to find other people living in them, quite happily; all the furniture had been taken; the books, diplomas, letters, photographs were gone. He found that under law he still owned his house. An eager lawyer told him of how it could easily be regained. Leon thought for a moment and then simply said, "What would I do with it?" and walked out.

He went to photographers in the neighborhood to try to find a photograph of his wife or his parents. They made him pay exorbitantly to search through their files. Thousands of men, women, and children stared out at him, but he found nothing. He had been arrested and his papers had been confiscated. Because of that he hadn't even a picture, or signature, or anything at all of his wife or parents. He remembered his father in the station, in his jacket. Where was his jacket?

He went to friends to inform them that he was alive and to seek information. They had none. He did not wish to hear of his mother and father, for they were dead and there was no point in reconstructing those days when he had been absent. But Ann was still alive. Of this he was convinced, since there was no record of her anywhere. No one had seen her, her name was to be found on no lists, there were no rumors.

It was said that beautiful women survived better than anyone else and he hoped for this. She might have been in England, Russia, France, America, Palestine, anywhere. People in the camps were going to Palestine. He knew that she might not even have been able to return to France, and hoped that she had been in Palestine all during the war. On the train they had discussed it, for although their first choice was America they knew they had no chance of entry. He spent weeks and months imagining her healthy and dark, farming the land and changed. And anyway, although he loved Europe he could not bear to put one foot down after another there. He left for Palestine from Trieste, illegally, but by then he had a talent for such things.

The Mediterranean—bright and dark, covered with mists of glowing air, surrounded by coasts of white rock and fish-eating cities, divided by islands of pine and citrus, rapid carrier of heat and conflict—enlivened him for a time. Three weeks on the deck of an old ship, with men and women as broken, defeated, and numb as the rusting iron and toothless rails, made him aware of his strength once again. He was moving once more, as rapidly as when he had fallen into France by silken parachute, or followed an armored column across the Rhine. These wretched refugees even sang, and despite its age the ship went forward, and the waves went eastward, waves which would become a new state, sweeping through it as it grew. They sang "My Thoughts Are Free," and they sang "The Day Will Come," and many other songs, so that at night on the small ship by yellow lantern light the new state took shape, in waves of feeling and energy, like a song. The children were given life, born here. And Leon, who had begun to crumble, had a part of him braced. He was again in the deep flux of history, nurtured only by events and hopes. The sun rose and beat upon the green sea. It set, and left its mark of bronze and red on the faces of those who had cast their eyes always to the East. I love, he thought, I must love. If I cannot love Maman, and Papa, and Ann, then I must at least love this land a little.

And the days passed as they hid behind islands and kept off the sea lanes until one late afternoon as the sun lit the East they found themselves, gasping as if at a stage play, face to face with land on which waves broke hard. A hot sweet wind came off the beaches and mountains. They could see trees ashore. They were face to face with the cliffs of Rosh HaNikra, and the British awaited them with trucks and lights while doglike patrol boats made wakes in lariats and loops and figure eights across their bows and off their stern. They were to be detained. But some decided to take to the water.

Leon was the first. As part of his training in England before he was sent into France he had to swim a mile every day. After many months of delays he became an excellent swimmer—much more so than he had been, and he had been good. He decided to swim around the British cordon. Although loudspeakers said he would drown, and some unfortunates did, he knew it was just a question of a few hours in the water. He tied his shoes around his neck and jumped into the sea. A second later he felt a splash beside him and from a froth of white emerged a girl's head. She said in Italian, since that was the language of the ship, "To swim beyond, no?" and he just began. They started straight north, parallel to the shore. She kept on wanting to go in, but he insisted that they clear the cordon and land where the cliffs came down to the sea. "That's dangerous," said the girl swimmer, who was about twenty. "Exactly," he replied, "there will be no police dogs there."

The waves were crashing against the rock as if in a great storm, and some of them flowed into caves where their breaking was trumpeted to the sea. It was getting dim when they made for a large cave, thinking to hide in it for the night and then swim out the next day. The entrance was narrow and surrounded with sharp rocks. They centered themselves as best they could and were swept inwards, almost crashing on a wall of rock. They swam for a while

until they reached the back of the grotto and a ledge
to which the water reached out and then receded
gently. They climbed out and found themselves in
a roaring mist. The air was wetter than the sea, the
rock salty and moist. In the remaining light he looked
at his companion and discovered a beautifully pro-
portioned, darkly tanned half-naked girl. They were
exhausted; the waves, noise, and depth of the cave
were counters to inhibition. They had after all accomplished a great feat and they were landed. They
stared at one another, both of them trembling from
the hours of swimming, and she slowly wrung out her
shirt. It was in fact a dream situation, but he rapidly
found himself feeling nothing. His greater loyalties
surfaced as if from the sea. He just stared at her, his
heart contained by an open question. All was cold,
and dead, and over. He would not marry ever again,
or make love, or fall in love. Such would ruin his
chances. He simply could not take certain breaths,
for fear of toppling Ann into hopelessness. What had
she apart from his faith? So he stared dully at this girl
who truly was able to impart deliriousness, and the
night passed miserably. If he had felt temptation, and
if he had felt longing for Ann, they had mixed to become as clean, smooth, and monotonous as the moist
green stone which had been ground down by the
waves.

Before dawn broke he had passed through many an
ecstasy and sustained many a second wind. But with
the coming of the light he felt drained and quiet,
breathing hard and slowly like the dove. He feared
that it had been chilled when the fire burned down,

and overheated when he built it up again. It looked so much, in its expression, like a human invalid, that he found himself sometimes imagining that he was by the bed of a sick child. But he glanced at its Oriental luminescence, the warmest of colors, reminding him that it was indeed a dove and that he had chosen to remain by its side waiting despite the consequences.

He had sometimes exercised his wants despite consequences and tugged at the patience of friends, if they could be called that. Unbelievably, he shirked guard duty for a decade or more, being allowed to do so because of his reputation as an intense eccentric. It was not that he wished to avoid work, for work was the only thing left to him, but rather that he genuinely feared to stand watch. He thought the crucial seconds between his sentry's challenge and a response would be wasted and that he might be killed. This was because he knew he would not shoot a shadow moving toward him on a moon or star lit night, thinking it might be Ann, come to find him.

She had long ago assumed these proportions, of a shadow or a shade, a walker on the floor of the valley without touching it, a descender from the deep sky, pale and sad, a ghost, a weeping gossamer, as white as powder and as quiet. This was unavoidable, a debt to pay, for in his stronger imaginings she was red as all life, moving, bursting into laughter, singing, fighting him, loving him—and imagination's pendulum had to sway.

When he had first come to the Bet Shan Valley he

had found, as if in coordination with everything else, that the climate was unbearable and the land an infested swamp. But he worked hard to clear it where it was not already cleared. For him it was as if the more beautiful the valley became the more likely that she would suddenly arrive. There was always the faintest hope, like one star on a black night, which sometimes in his dreams became a wall of white light blinding him with happiness as if the next day he would see her, for one never knew. These, while they lasted, were his best times, although extraordinarily bitter afterwards.

And yet his dreams did not run in place. He knew that everything moves forward, and he had grown and developed despite himself over the years. A film which in 1950 or 1960 had seemed to him to be richer and fuller than life itself, and certainly as real, was upon re-showing no more authoritative as to the depth of things than a fast-moving montage of African and Asian postage stamps—colorful and interesting, but with the flow and humanity of a cogwheel. Things moved forward, and although most of his life had been the history of solitude, a long unbroken color, and although his wisdom had served only to heighten the quality of his sadness, he continued to think that perhaps there would be a day when his unraveled life would again be whole.

The practice of years on the land made him look up. On a distant hill he saw horses and riders in the heat of middle morning, raising threads of dust. They would soon be upon him. He looked at the dove, its eyes three-quarters closed, and surmised that despite its gentleness it was willed to die.

And what would the horsemen say, seeing him beside a dove dying rapidly on a palm branch he had cut? These young men would not understand. They did not know what he thought and felt. He was beyond their concern and that was in his view quite right. For they had to grow up and pass their scores of years and enter into history. They too would be old, touched by events younger ones could not understand. They too would go to their graves alone, obsessed with remembrances of a life which in its incredible variation had pushed them out beyond the society of men into quiet places where they could only reflect. Starting on the surface of a sphere, crowded and touching, each man moved outwards so that the longer his life the greater the loneliness around him. Nothing can be done, and there is no comfort in it. There is no comfort in dying, no comfort in growing old. In the end there is no solace even in history. But a young man and an old man are moved before they die to finish the task of their life. And this, Leon, far from Paris and far from his love, could do.

A pair of horsemen came down a near hill, raising dust in the white morning sun. They were approaching the grove of trees. Leon looked at the motionless dove, and then at the horses and men galloping toward him.

The gentleness of a dove is something we cannot understand. Sometimes a fighter, it is not all of one color. But most of all it is moved by quiet love and a wish for simple life among the trees. And when it dies it breaks us apart, for it never thinks of itself. But God protect it if it should die alone, and God protect its poor family.

MARK HELPRIN

Read his short stories. They will "delight, open, and elevate you."*

Lose yourself in the hands of a master storyteller, a consummate artist whose short stories have been described as dazzling, brilliant, and breathtaking.

—— **A DOVE OF THE EAST & Other Stories**
32151-4-37 $3.95

—— **ELLIS ISLAND & Other Stories**
32204-9-18 $3.95

*The Baltimore Sun